SOLID

Clio Kaid may be 17 and just beginning the last summer before her senior year, but her life is anything but typical.

She's just discovered she was genetically altered before birth and is now headed to a top-secret Army campus to explore the surprising results of the experiment.

Follow Clio and the other teens as they develop fantastic super-abilities, forge new friendships, find love, and uncover a conspiracy along the way.

PRAISE FOR "SOLID"

This is a great story for MG and YA readers, and fans of James Patterson's Maximum Ride series will enjoy the adventures of this new group of kids who are just a little 'different.'   ~ Book Noise

On first seeing the cover and reading the summary, I thought that "Solid" would be something new, different, and intriguing - and it was.
~ Between the Covers

Reading its summary will unquestionably get you interested. And reading its contents will get you hooked and addicted.
~ Reading Lassie

Ms. Workinger is worthy of her own place in the science-fiction/fantasy genre, because this really is an original and stand-out novel.
~ Magic of Reading

Brimming with entertaining, loyal characters, a gripping, mysterious back story/plot, teens with superhuman abilities, and a satisfying ending that cleverly paves the way for a pine-worthy sequel.
~ Paranormal Indulgence

If I had to describe "Solid" in one line, it would be - YA version of Robin Cook novels but much more fun and exciting!
~ My Love Affair With Books

Readers who would like a sci-fi adventure with a heroine that is real and realistic rather than a knock-off of a cable TV channel vixen, this is the story for you!   ~ Litland

A hint of romance, a splash of mystery, and the superhero powers that they are just coming into, and you have yourself an entertaining, and page-turning read. No sex and no swearing, so even the younger tweens may enjoy this one.   ~ Minding Spot

While the plot might be the foundation of this story, its characters were the heart of it.   *~ Escape Between the Pages*

"Solid" is a wonderful book that brings in a batch of fascinating characters and an intriguing plot that will keep you guessing.
                                    ~ Confessions of a Bookaholic

It's always a good indication when you like the main character immediately.   *~ One Book At A Time*

The story line is very entertaining with a cast of quirky, loveable and memorable characters…comic relief as well as romance. If you like the X-men or Heroes, I think you will like this book.
                                    ~ To Read or Not to Read

A different approach to geeky-high-school-girl-turns-special.
                                    ~ A Musing Reviews

I fell in love with her characters and had no difficulty completely immersing myself into "Solid." An amazing read that is enticing and captivating. It kept me gripped from the first place to the last. I highly recommend this book!   *~ My Bookish Fairytale*

This was a solid (no pun intended) story, and I'm definitely interested in reading the sequel "Settling" when I can get my hands on it.
                                    ~ Royal Reviews

I honestly think that for a book that is as good as it is, I don't think it will get the full attention that it truly deserves.   *~ Reading Chic*

The story moves at a fast-pace and the characters come to life in a way that will have readers caring about them. I devoured this book in just a couple of days.   *~ Socrates' Book Reviews*

SOLID

SOLID

Printed in the United States of America

Third Edition

For my brilliant friends,
who used their own special
super-abilities to make
this dream a reality.

PROLOGUE

As per his nighttime routine, he checked the security panel to ensure that the system would alert him of any intrusions on the perimeter he'd set around the lab. The doctor was putting in a late night, also consistent with his normal regimen, successfully employing the strategy of hiding in plain sight.

After engaging the lock and closing the blinds over the glass door, he crouched behind his desk, feeling around the legs until he'd released each of the four latches holding it in place. It was easy then to slide the desk two and a half feet toward the door and expose the hatch while still keeping it concealed from anyone entering the room, not that there was any real possibility of a visitor.

Next, he unlocked the bottom left drawer of the desk, removing a brown leather journal and replacing it with the Army service garrison he'd pulled from his head. He took care to

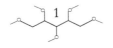

collapse the cap along the crease, the polished silver eagle pinned to the top. Although *Colonel* was undoubtedly a commendable distinction, he did consider the PhD at the other end of his name the more honorific of his titles. But he didn't need reminding that both ranks were necessary to conduct his ground-breaking research. He released the rope ladder at the top of the opening, paused for one more visual sweep, and made his descent.

Once his feet landed on the concrete floor, his hand reached out automatically to flip the wall switch. The fluorescent hum was quickly drowned out by the scurrying of little feet against glass and shavings as the inhabitants of the repurposed bunker came to life. *Roll call*, as he liked to think of it, began to the immediate right of his entry point and would proceed clockwise around the four walls – forty-eight feet of cages stacked three high.

He flipped to the next blank page in his journal, almost at the end of this eighteenth volume of copious notes, and used the standard issue *Get The Lead Out* ball-point to tap a friendly greeting on the glass of specimen 92-9A13. His tiny, whiskered subject hardly needed encouragement; he was literally bouncing off the walls – and ceiling – of his cage as if the floor was made of rubber.

"Take it easy, Jordan," the doctor chuckled in a fatherly tone as he let his eyes pass briefly over the mouse's equally

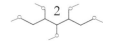

buoyant neighbors. Though their freakish agility would have astounded anyone else, it failed to merit more than a passing glance from their designer. These, his earliest and most successful creations, were well-established and gave him no surprise. They were ready.

He continued past a stretch of clean and empty cages before reaching the next section. The specimens along this second wall earned the same friendly but tepid response as he'd given the others, though their eerie stillness stood in sharp contrast to group one. The only movement came from furry subject 92-9171 who, while showing no reaction to the human observer, continued tapping out a heavy rhythm along the back wall with her tail. The doctor followed her unwavering rodent gaze to the spitting serpent at the far end of her cage. Instead of feeling guilty for having forgotten to put back her safety wall, his eyes glittered with anticipation. The smooth, black snake first coiled to attack, then dove forward to strike, only to stop an inch short of its target as if blocked by an unseen force.

If his hands hadn't been full of pen and journal, the doctor would've clapped his hands in approval. Instead, he rewarded her defensive maneuver with a rare bit of compassion. "Let's give you a night of rest, my Ludi," he said, and dropped a partition down the center of the cage to separate the combatants. The denied viper continued to spit in the mouse's direction, but

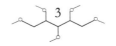

her opponent had already curled up in a protective ball to recuperate from the extended period of intense concentration.

"I know you're in there," the doctor called teasingly as he next approached group three – a line of seemingly unoccupied cages. His ears perked up immediately at the rustling response and he bent at the waist to peer into a cage on the lowest level marked 92-9M129. His eyes lit up to see the shavings part as if by an invisible breeze. "Ah, Griffin, there you are," he purred, tracing one finger down the glass and making a brief rubbing gesture near the disturbed spot. "I know you hate being woken up at night, but you know how much I love not seeing you." He laughed at his own private joke.

It was then with near giddiness that he proceeded to the fourth section, quickly closing the journal and placing it atop 92-9Q224. He put his hands on either side of the glass enclosure to peer within, intent as if searching the gaze of his beloved. The shimmering creature inside nearly took his breath away and he absently stroked the enclosure as he cooed, "You're going to blind Dr. Heigl one of these days, Siri." She was his prize, his crowning achievement, his *star*. It took several minutes for him to tear his eyes away from her, straighten up, and reclaim his journal.

Like a love-struck boy at the end of a dance, he backed toward the exit, reluctant to leave and end the enchanted evening. It was only after he'd placed a hand on the ladder that he realized

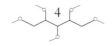

he'd overlooked someone. He turned back to address the lone occupied cage to his immediate left, 87-9X.

"Hey, didn't mean to pass you by, little man." The gray mouse sat up on its hind legs to lock beady eyes as the doctor continued, "It's time, old friend. They're ready." He made a sweeping gesture to include all of the other subjects and ended with a winking salute. Then he turned back toward the exit, hit the lights, and climbed up.

After deftly replacing the desk to camouflage the secret door and once again securing the journal in the locked drawer, he looked up and caught his reflection in the window glass. He jauntily flicked his stiff cap with one finger, his mouth widening in a fiendish grin as he unabashedly admired the face of the soon-to-be most revered geneticist in, not just military or medical, but, in fact, *world* history.

ONE

*D*_{*ay one, take fifty,*} I self-narrated, pausing in the open doorway. My stomach fluttered in the same sort of day-one vu that I felt at each new school debut. I braced myself for the predictable newbie interrogation - *What's your name? Where're you from? Are you even worth talking to, or should I move on?*

I'd learned a long time ago to be wary of the early-greeters – the attention-seekers who latched on right away to ensure that no attention would be drawn away from them. Also to look out for were the outcasts looking for in-crowd admission to whom my forehead marquee apparently announced "Backstage Pass."

Just stop, Calliope Grace, my mother's voice sounded in my head and a red octagon appeared as a solid block in my thought path. I wasn't a negative person, but, despite all efforts to stop them, sarcastic quips always seemed to win the word race from my mind to my mouth. In truth, I was kind of looking forward to this day – to walking into a new room of unknown faces and opportunities. Not everyone gets the chance to start a new life pretty much every year, and I'd learned it could be interesting for those willing to embrace it.

Besides all the feelings I knew would bubble up today, like always – the hope to make a connection with a new friend, then the worry that once I got attached to that friend it'd be time to move and I'd only ever see them again on Facebook – this was actually a whole new scenario for me. Where I was used to being the only new person in a sea of kids who'd known each other since kindergarten, here *everyone* was new. We'd each been invited to this campus designed especially for us, and I wondered how it would all play out. Would everyone gravitate toward the usual high school cliques? Or the opposite – each kid a loner with no pre-set groups to move into or away from.

I stepped forward, not a hard move to make with so much practice. In fact, the only *un*expected part of this unprecedented situation was the part that was exactly like a typical first day of school - I had to go in on my own. When I'd been told I was headed for a classified government facility in the middle of nowhere, I'd assumed my mom would be with me. I mean, obviously, as seventeen-year-olds, we'd all be perfectly

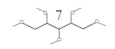

capable of registering, getting the layout, figuring out what we needed to do, and ignoring what we knew was nonsensical. I just wasn't used to adults giving us that much credit and letting the leash out so far. *But,* I rationalized, *I guess a military-run camp probably has its own special form of supervision.*

Even my handler-slash-bodyguard-slash-travel buddy had disappeared after depositing me in the lobby with only the instruction to report to the main hall for my entry interview. Lieutenant Graham had explained to me on the plane up here to Jersey from New Orleans this morning that, instead of checking into our rooms first like at a hotel, we'd each meet with a staff member to be "sorted out." *Ha, bring on the singing hat, right?* And although I now found myself wishing I had a bit more intel on the campus, at the time I'd just been relieved that the lieutenant wasn't a big talker. The last thing I'd wanted to do this morning was dig for small talk, and the down time on the flight had definitely contributed to the relative calm I was feeling now.

"Name?" The sharp inflection on the single word gave away the door-greeter's military status even though she, like the rest of the staff, was not in uniform.

So much for taking my time and feeling my way around, I groaned inwardly, also dismayed that she'd apparently missed last Saturday's press conference about this place – that it was supposed to be run by the *kinder, gentler* military. Since I got the

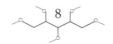

feeling it may have actually killed her to look up from her clipboard and smile, I just followed her lead.

"Kaid, Clio," I informed her dutifully. My response was met with a wrinkled forehead as she futilely scanned the page.

"Or Calliope, I guess," I amended, trying not to grimace at the name that pretty much only existed on my birth certificate.

"Miss Kaid," she acknowledged curtly without meeting my eyes and her owl-like head swiveled to examine the room behind her. "You may proceed to table twelve."

I wanted to ask if she was aware there were no big numbers painted on the dozen or so identical tables in the large room, but instead I bit my tongue as a reminder to behave. Following the general direction of her gaze, I spotted one woman facing an empty seat and figured that must be where I needed to go. I shrugged my shoulder-bag further toward the back of my hip to maneuver between the other tables and chairs until I reached my destination.

"Good morning; have a seat. Thirsty?" As I put my bag down on the floor by the chair opposite her, the woman waiting for me used her pen to indicate the pitcher and matching glasses at the side of our table. Her genuine smile – with teeth and everything – was a hugely positive sign after the non-welcome by Bouncer Bertha. I readily smiled back and helped myself to some water, surprised to find real glass and not paper dentist-office

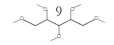

cups. Either eco-awareness was part of this new Army, or dish duty would be the penance for bad behavior.

"Calliope," my processor began, but quickly and impressively caught what was surely recoil on my face and rephrased. "Not Calliope – you have a nickname you prefer."

"Everyone calls me Clio, thanks." I studied her a bit as she made a quick note of this. She was older than me – obviously, she'd have to be to work this post – but younger than I'd expected. Funkier, too, with dark hair razor-edged from short at the back to graduated fringe around her face. Even her squarish black glasses were trendy – first-season Sylar-ish.

"Got it," she smiled again. "I'm Janet Quirk. As I'm sure you've figured out, I work for the Department of Defense and I'm part of the team they called in to staff this facility where we, shall we say, will attempt to make up for the *unfortunate incident* that affected all of you. The more hands-on officers, like myself, are here to help you find your way through this self-exploratory period and do anything we can to ease the process for you. For now, we're kind of referring to ourselves as *guides*."

I nodded so she knew I was listening. This was basically the same as what Lieutenant Graham had said when he'd arrived at my house last week and dropped what was then a bomb about a rogue genetic experiment conducted by the military eighteen years ago. Weirdly enough, the shock had almost fully diffused

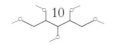

for me by this point.

"To be honest," she began, and if it were anybody else, I would've laughed out loud – *when an adult says they're about to be honest, it's usually followed by a load of crap* – but Janet Quirk wasn't rubbing me that way. "We don't know a whole lot." And now she was the funny, cynical one. "I know we usually don't admit that as a collective but, hey, you've heard the party line – *old secrets, new light*," she said, turning both open palms face up. "That's the deal. We're going to be frank about the things we don't know and work with you to find the truth. It's all we can do. C9x is what we're calling the project, by the way," she added. "*C9* for chromosome nine, the one you had altered, and *x* for experiment or something like that. You get the point."

"Maybe the *x* is for *x-factor*?" I offered with a smile, and was rewarded with a great grin in return.

"Exactly. So, as you know," she went on, "the C9x experiment was conducted in absolute secrecy, and was aborted when the officer behind it died. Since he'd worked alone, virtually all knowledge of C9x died with him. If an informant hadn't recently come forward with a manifest of the pregnant women who'd been given the unknown drug, we may never have known. Pretty much all we've been able to put together is which chromosome Dr. Heigl targeted. You kids are our only hope of discovering the purpose of his work."

11

And just like four days ago, we'd reached the part for me that was the hardest to swallow. High school and teenage life were tricky enough to navigate without looking for some random deformity in me to make things even harder. I'd never sat down and picked myself apart, but now I was having a hard time doing anything else.

"I'll do whatever you think will help," I assured her, "but I don't have any kind of body problems that I know of." In truth, I'd been fairly biologically fortunate up to this point – dark red hair nowhere near the shade of any root vegetable, not the first or last in my grade to get boobs, and a decent metabolism that let me eat a Snickers if I felt like it. *All in all, pretty lucky. Until now.*

"It's becoming pretty clear to us that none of your outward appearances have suffered. Actually," she lowered her voice to confide with a wink, "the group as a whole is quite good-looking. But that should have no correlation to C9x, so for all intents and purposes we're going to chalk it up to coincidence for now. If it ever becomes relevant, we can always revisit."

"And although we have significantly more girls than boys," she continued, offering an unnecessary but appreciated observation, "the drugs were administered to women who were already pregnant, so that's probably another unrelated fluke. What I can tell you is that we believe the drug you were given affects mainly muscles and tissues – essentially the meaty parts of you between your skin and bones. There's a host of terminology I could throw at you, but I couldn't pronounce half of it and you're going to have a fairly thorough lecture tomorrow anyway. For now, we're referring to this affected dimension as your *solidity*."

Again, all I could do was nod – it wasn't like I had any great insight to contribute.

"Anyway, what we'd like to hear from you would be any out-of-the-norm physical experiences you may have had," she explained. "Anything you can think of as far as your strength or flexibility that you've noticed may be different or unique."

"I'm not really a sports kind of girl," I answered almost guiltily, starting to wonder if there may not be a place for me in this project after all.

"That's fine, Clio." Her eyes, clear and bright, met mine. "Remember, there's no wrong answer. You're one of the victims and now it's *our* responsibility to make things right for *you*." She paused and then tried a new angle, "Can you think of a time when something should have come easy to you, but you couldn't do it at all? Or, conversely, were you ever able to do something you shouldn't have been able to?"

"Like a superpower?" I asked, seriously not trying to be sarcastic.

"More like an action you might've attributed to an adrenalin rush, or to momentum and luck. Like this – one of the

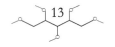

boys I interviewed this morning plays baseball and consistently catches hits that should've been home runs. So, is he just that good, or could there be something more to it?"

"Nothing like that for me." I assured her, letting out a small laugh under my breath.

"That laugh," she called me out. "You're thinking of something."

"I was just thinking about my dreams and how they work...," I started and stopped, but her eyes shone so expectantly that I went on with my ridiculous-ness anyway. "I'll be having a nightmare where I'm being chased by a murderer – or a vampire, or whatever – but then I stop and say to myself, *I'm invisible; he can't see me.* Then I can still see myself, but whoever's after me runs right by like I vanished. And I watch it all happen, like I'm outside my body or something." I flushed, feeling the need to add, "You asked."

"I did, and you answered perfectly," she assured me. "I meant what I said before, that you should go ahead and say how you feel. Just give me everything you've got and I'll take it from there."

My cheeks cooled back down as she made another brief note on her yellow pad. *How old school,* I noted. *We're almost in the twenty-tens and they don't even get laptops?*

"I think we're off to a good start here with your profile,"

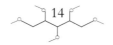

she said, calling me back from my thoughts. "I don't feel the need to torture you any further. Today, at least." She smiled warmly as she pushed back her chair, rose to her feet, and extended a hand. I got up, too, shouldering my bag with my left hand and extending my right to shake hers, impressed by the respectful gesture as I was more used to being dismissed by authority figures.

"It was great meeting you," she said, concluding our talk. "Next you'll want to join everybody else in the dining hall for dinner. Have a good time – we think you're going to be a great group."

"Thanks," I answered and headed toward the double doors on the opposite side of the room from where I'd come in, wondering what I'd be walking into next.

TWO

I lingered in the doorway, surveying the dining room to formulate an entry strategy. I found the space as equally unexceptional as the last – bright and clean, plain and institutional. Even the buzzing groups of kids were no different than in any other cafeteria at any other school. So it made sense for me to act the same as always, too. Normally, that'd mean choosing an empty table to leave my books on and then going to get my food, but right now all I had to mark my place was my purse, which my mom taught me to never let out of my sight in mixed company. I finally decided to assemble a meal first and hope that a good seating choice would reveal itself by the time I was ready to sit.

There were standard plastic trays just inside the door, but I soon saw that that was the only similarity to a regular cafeteria. To begin with, there were no obvious lines of any kind. Instead, the food was spread over five stations, each its own island of available fare. First came a salad bar; next a "ball park" grouping of burgers, hot dogs, fries and chicken fingers; then a dozen pizza choices; followed by a home-cooked meal of the day; and, lastly, a pyramid of plated desserts. All the neatly labeled items waited in covered metal warming pans or in iced trays, pointing out the second anomaly – no servers.

Another quick scan of the room confirmed that there were no adult monitors of any kind. *Maybe they're serious about keeping it casual*, I thought to myself. I knew I, for one, was going to feel much more at ease here if not under oppressive supervision.

I took a tray and began to wander around the dinner options. The fries did look fresh and crispy, but the thought of the lead-gut feeling I'd suffer from later propelled me past the entire fried section. Maybe because it was my first night away from home, the home-style dinner called to me the most – spaghetti with a thick, meaty sauce and garlic bread to seal the deal. The accompanying vegetable – Brussels sprouts – was not for me, but I responsibly made my way back to the salad bar for something green to balance out the colors on my plate.

Just as I tonged a bunch of fresh broccoli, an orange buzzed by my ear and soared up over my head, followed quickly by an apple, then a banana. Clutching my tray, I ducked back out of the produce storm, trying to figure out where it was coming from.

"I wouldn't have hit you; I have marksman precision," teased the lightly-dimpled, brown-haired boy as each fruit returned to his cupped hands with soft thump, thump, thumps.

I opened my mouth to lob back a clever retort, or even a decent compliment on his skill, but found myself struck embarrassingly dumb.

Luckily for me, he filled the gap. "It's the banana that impressed you, right? Anyone can juggle round fruits but you need real talent for odd shapes. I'm Jack by the way." He held up the fruits to excuse his lack of handshake offer.

"Clio," I replied, mimicking the gesture with my own full tray and realizing that I felt strangely disappointed. I started myself by thinking how I wanted nothing more at that moment than to know if his hands were as warm and soft as his dark brown eyes. But I also knew his touch would surely turn me into a complete blithering idiot.

"Cleo? As in Queen of the Nile?" he asked, proving he was not just ridiculously cute but also intriguingly literary – a combination much more thrilling than the usual good-looking face painted on a hollow rock. *Plus the juggling? Seriously hot.*

"Clio, as in a big stretch of a nickname for Calliope." Better late than never, my voice finally made its appearance. "But

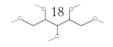

we can keep that detail confidential." Even if this extraordinary guy was into it, the last thing I wanted was to be saddled with that clunker of a moniker in this new crowd.

"Calliope's a great name," he responded in earnest. "One of the nine beautiful muses, right?"

As if, I thought, shocked. *He knows Greek mythology and likes my name, too?* This was obvious proof that the genetic experiment had indeed caused wild mutations.

"Even my parents, who chose the fabulous name, have never actually called me by it," I assured him, at the same time thinking how impressed I was that he even knew how to pronounce it. I was used to horribly mangled attempts like *Cal-ee-oh-pay* - a great name for a Spanish rodeo clown.

"Clio's cool, too," he went on, "and another muse, I'm pretty sure."

In my mind I may have said, *I'll be sure of anything you are*, but aloud I answered, "I guess that's why your performance was so *inspired*." I was quite pleased with myself for finally throwing up some wit points on my side of the board.

Jack rolled his eyes in mock distaste for the bad pun, so I took the opportunity to flip the focus to him. "So is Jack short for anything – John? Jackson?"

"Just Jack," he said again with that killer grin, and I was glad to see him drop the fruit onto a tray instead of tossing it

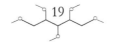

back onto the salad bar after being man-handled.

Now came the awkward part where nicctics wcre used up, the food-getting was over, and we either needed to sit and eat together or part ways. I was pretty sure I'd exhausted my allotment of sparkling conversation for the day so I looked around, casually planning my exit.

I knew immediately that I wanted to avoid the raven-haired girl to the far left – the one shooting daggers at anyone who drifted within shouting distance of her table while at the same time manically shredding a poor defenseless round of pita bread with her angry black finger-talons. An about-face to my right revealed a table of pre-frat boys launching grape grenades into each other's mouths. Then, like a mirage, I spotted, in the middle, two open, encouraging smiles.

Jack must have noticed them at the same time because he said, "Looks like they've got room."

For both of us? How have I possibly not scared you off yet? I thought, then followed his lead with a new determination to get myself together.

Suddenly, the red sauce on my plate was no longer looking like the best choice, but I was definitely not going to be one of those weird girls who won't eat in front of guys. The guy thinks you're freaky while you sit there all hungry and crabby – totally a lose-lose. I was tempted to mummify myself with

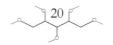

napkins in a sad attempt to save the – *what else?* – white, embroidered-eyelet tee that was supposed to be one of my staples for the summer. I silently debated, *Which is worse – toddler or slob?* I made a silent promise to be maximum-level careful as I sat down and greeted my tablemates.

"Hi," from the girl and "Hey," from the guy rang out at the same time. He chivalrously nodded that she should handle the introductions.

"I'm Bliss." She may have gotten the short-end of the name stick, too, but fate had certainly overcompensated in making it up to her with long, spun-gold hair and bright grape-green eyes. I'd have written her off right away if she hadn't eyed my plate wistfully and said, "I wish I had your nerve. I couldn't have even made it to the table without wearing that." I felt instantly guilty for unfairly judging her and knew we were going to be fast friends.

"I'm Garrett." Her cohort was also easy on the eyes – well over six feet tall and a sandier blond with a strong and lean athletic build. "And I think you two rolling in spaghetti would be hot." *Pervy, but funny – he could grow on me.*

"This is Clio and I'm Jack," As usual, I'd been doing more thinking than talking, so it was nice of him to throw me the line.

"Oh, did y'all know each other before?" Bliss looked back

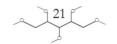

and forth between us expectantly.

"No, I just tried to pick her up at the salad bar but apparently my A-game wasn't good enough since she made a bee-line for this joker," Jack grinned at Garrett.

"Watch and learn, my brother. You can call me the Master of Attraction – or just Master, as long as you bow." Garrett's confident retort to Jack was all cute, none cocky, and I was glad for the deflection away from me. And I loved that the two boys seemed to be hitting it off as well as Bliss and I were. This was by far the smoothest first day I'd ever had.

"So where are y'all from?" Bliss, the good hostess, returned to her welcoming-committee duties.

"Oklahoma – Fort Still," Garrett threw out first. "You're all looking at the finest first baseman to ever come out of Lawton, by the way."

"Try to remember that you knew us way back when." My words and eye roll came out reflexively before I realized I'd unknowingly stepped up for my turn. "New Orleans," I gave my home city and was met with puzzlement times three, so I quickly filled in, "We're civilians, me and my mom. My dad died when I was a baby, so no more bases for us."

"I'm so sorry," Bliss clearly felt bad and I instantly regretted being a downer.

Thankfully, Garrett was quick to find the positive. "Hey,

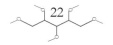
22

at least you didn't have to move all the time, right?"

"Actually, my mom's a writer so we moved a lot when she was first getting started and 'finding her voice.' Once she kind of got established we bought a house, but we're still on the road a lot for her book tours."

"That sounds awesome," Jack enthused. "Getting to go everywhere you want without being stuck anywhere."

"It is pretty great," I agreed, but I also didn't want to keep monopolizing the conversation. I nudged Bliss with my elbow and teased her about her not-so-subtle accent, "You must have come up from somewhere south, too."

"All over, pretty much," she answered. "We started in El Paso, did the full Southeast circuit and ended up last year back in Texas at Sam Houston. It should be my mom's last move."

"Wait, is your mom…," Jack started to make a connection but was cut off by a new arrival to our table.

"Hello, people. Miranda Taylor." Another beautiful blonde on par with Bliss sat down as if invited, then proceeded to challenge her manicure by peeling an avocado. "Carry on your convo," she ordered an end to the silence she'd brought on.

"We were just all saying where we're from," Bliss hesitantly filled the gap, looking around for someone to take the baton.

"North Carolina," Jack started, but before he could

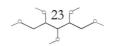

follow up with "Fort Bragg," the others called out simultaneously, "Been there." Even I knew that Bragg was a huge base and most of the kids in this room had probably done time there at some point.

"Well, I'm at Irwin, and my skin is desperately missing the California air. I don't know how you people live like this." Looked like Miranda certainly wasn't the shy, quiet type.

"Like what?" I asked, though not defensively as I wouldn't even know what to be defensive about.

She indignantly tossed down the last quarter of green rind and addressed me like a child. "First of all, there's no humidity here; I can feel the fault lines spreading across my face."

"Um," Garrett had no qualms about interrupting the interrupter. "Isn't Irwin in the Mojave Desert? As in all dry, all the time?"

"The base is, but we don't live *there*," she retorted with such distaste it was like he'd accused her of living in a cardboard box on the side of the road. "We live in the mountains in Big Bear Lake. My dad has to commute like two hours each way, but it's so worth it. Anyway, back to what I was saying – the East Coast smoxins are blackening our lungs as we speak." When she was greeted with a collective non-response, she delivered her summation, "Our bodies are temples, folks. I, for one, plan to preserve mine exquisitely, not just let it rot and get all old and nasty."

Unfortunately, any validity in her point was kind of lost in the shadow of her pissy attitude. As I tried to find the most diplomatic way to tell her so, all eyes at the table looked up to focus over my head.

I turned in my seat to find a tall, dad-aged man in a sports coat and khakis standing right behind me. As soon as he began to speak, I recognized him from the press conference as Colonel Randall Clark, director of this project.

"Is everyone enjoying their dinner?" His fatherly smile swept the group to acknowledge each of us. "We snagged the old White House chef and his staff when the last president left office." He lifted his eyebrows with self-pride. "We heard the Bush twins loved his cheeseburger pizza and tuna hummus wraps so we figured, keep the menu for the girls, triple the quantity for the boys, and everyone'll be happy."

"Wow." "Great." "Okay." All of us tried to respond politely, but the moment was still awkward. We couldn't tell if he was just making the rounds or if he wanted something from us.

I shouldn't have even *mentally* asked, because as soon as the thought crossed my mind, I felt his bear paw land firmly on the back of my chair.

"Calliope Kaid?" He looked down at me and I felt my stomach turn over. "I'd like to speak with you in my office."

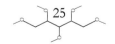

There was an awkward pause, then he finished, "The rest of you have a good night."

When he turned and started walking away, I dutifully followed, abandoning the half-eaten meal that I no longer wanted anyway. I couldn't even look back to say goodnight to Bliss and the others, too embarrassed that I was being singled out for who knew what on the very first day.

THREE

Colonel Clark held the door for me and smiled encouragingly as I ducked under his arm and walked through. *At least he doesn't look mad*, I thought, hopefully.

"Please come in." His office was right off the foyer by the front entrance and he ushered me in, then closed the door behind him before assuming his seat on the other side of the desk. I tried to take in the room quickly before he got settled and found it easy to do so; aside from the desk chairs and twin bookshelves stocked with military manuals, there was nothing of note – no photos, no diplomas, not even a coat on the back of the door. I guessed I was going to have to trust my instincts in reading this guy as he sure didn't have any props to help me out.

"I'm sorry that I pulled you out of dinner," he began. "It looked like you were making some friends."

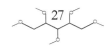

Trying to, at least, I muttered inwardly, but answered, "Yeah." I hated to be so non-responsive, but it was really all I had – no good response.

"I know this is stressful and somewhat confusing for all of us, but we're trying our best to make everything feel as normal as possible. That's why we started with the interviews – to get to know you a bit and not just assign everyone numbers and run some tests. What do you think?"

My thoughts were coming too fast and colliding in my tired brain. First of all, what did he mean by *us*? It's not like we were all in the same boat, since I was pretty sure all his chromosomes were happily intact. Second, was he really asking for my input? Was I supposed to say, *Yes, I get it. Brilliant strategy, Sir?* Or what I really thought, *You probably should've opened with some more background – like all of it – because we're kind of resentful that you haven't turned all the lights on yet.*

I didn't want to come off as rude and sarcastic when he seemed to be trying hard to speak to me like an intelligent human being, so I tried to go with lightly-humored honesty. Somewhat hesitantly I offered, "Things are off to an okay start. I appreciate not being strapped down and covered with electrodes and all, but it's all a little weird." *To say the least.*

"Of course," he rushed to sympathize.

"This is really the weirdest part of all, if you want to know

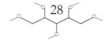

the truth," I blurted out, followed by, "Sorry." I saw right away that I'd hurt his feelings and hurried to try and explain myself better. "I mean, I don't know why you called me in here and I don't know what I'm supposed to tell you. Colonel. Sir." In other words, I still didn't know if I was in big trouble, or if I'd been selected to play the mole and spy on the other kids. And I wasn't okay with either possibility.

"No, I'm the one who should be sorry, Calliope," he apologized. "And please call me Randall."

My brain retorted, *I am so not doing that,* but I let him go on without interruption.

"I just wanted to officially introduce myself and let you know that I am available if you need anything. I thought you and your mother might feel better knowing you weren't completely alone here. I'm sure the separation must be hard on you both, since you're so close."

"Yes, we are…," I trailed off, not seeing what that had to do with him.

"You do understand why we decided it was best for everyone's parents to remain at home?" he asked, seeming again to be looking to me for confirmation.

"We were told it was to avoid the media and the crazies," I began, then decided to give him the opinion he'd asked for, "but I don't see how a hundred kids with armed soldiers arriving at the airport at the same time didn't look suspicious."

"Believe me, we considered all of the possibilities," he said, "and we felt that plain-clothed guards and a one soldier-one student ratio was the safest option."

In the ensuing pause I thought of one of my grandmother's old sayings – *In for a penny, in for a pound,* wasn't it? I heaved forward another loaded question, "Sir, why am I being singled out? I don't understand why I'm the only one you called in here."

"Damn, that was apparently another bad assumption on my part. I'm sure making a big mess of things," he said with a self-deprecating smile. "I thought you already knew who I was. Let me start over, then. I served with your father in the Gulf War, back before you were born and he…well, you know."

Before he died? My mind filled in his unspoken words. I wanted to say, *Just say it, I promise I won't lose it on you.*

Instead I stuck with, "Right, uh-huh." I tried to sound convincing since the fact that I should know him was ringing a faint bell, but, honestly, a lot of the guys from my dad's unit had contacted my mom and me over the years to make sure we were doing okay, or even just to reminisce about him, and I didn't really know one from the others. Thankfully, my mom had taken it for the team and spared me most of it.

"Your father was a great man," he began and, as his eyes

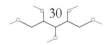

started to well up, I realized *I* wasn't the one he was worried about breaking down. "I was the combat medic in his unit," he continued, "so it was my job to take care of everyone. Luckily, we all made it home, but when we were over there, we promised each other that if anything happened to one of us, the rest would look out for the family left behind. That promise didn't end for me in the Gulf."

I was officially out of my comfort zone seeing such a statured man so unsettled. To me, John Kaid was more like a folklore character I knew only through pictures and stories. But I strangely felt like I should say something comforting to Colonel Clark. Of course, all I could think was, *Hey, I'm just a kid! Shouldn't you be talking to adults about this?*

He paused, to compose himself I assumed, and as I looked everywhere but at him, I was reminded that no, it didn't seem like he did have anyone. If he had a wife and kids, or even friends, there would probably be at least one photo on display.

"Anyway," he went on, his eyes thankfully clearing, his breathing slowed to mostly normal. "I just wanted to let you know you can call on me if you need to."

I really did appreciate the offer and didn't want to embarrass him by acting any more weirded-out, so I stood to make my exit. "Thank you very much, sir. And I'll let you know if anything comes up."

"Please do." He offered a firm hand and I shook it, echoing his good night while trying not to look too desperate for an escape. My mom had never been a griever, so his deep sadness felt like too heavy a burden for me to take on.

Not the most graceful exit, I self-lectured, *but at least it was quick.*

As I crossed the small courtyard from the mail building to what I'd been told was the residence hall, I took a deep breath and admired what I could see of the campus by the lamps lining the walk. I couldn't get over how, well, *green* New Jersey had turned out to be. I'd thought I was headed for the land of concrete, even though I'd been told numerous times that almost half the state was protected, undeveloped wild space. I'd even jokingly asked Lieutenant Graham on the way up why we weren't heading west to Area 51 where all the good secret stuff was hidden. He'd *non*-jokingly responded that the Jersey woods were pretty good for hiding things, too, and with better access to New York City. I didn't push my luck by asking if that was classified info or if he was going to have to kill me for knowing.

But now, looking up at an inky-black sky liberally sprinkled with stars, then down the treeline of towering oaks and thick pines with lush ferns tying it all to the ground, I could see why the locals kept the state's quiet beauty a secret. If I lived here, in this peace and tranquility, I wouldn't want more people moving in and ruining it for me, either.

And I wasn't the only one enjoying the perfect summer night. I didn't see anyone I recognized, but small clusters of kids sprawled across the benches, talking, and three guys were tossing around a Frisbee.

If I wasn't so completely exhausted, I would've loved to lay a blanket out on the grass and read by the warm orange glow of the lamps. Instead, I headed into the dorm, embarking on the four-flight climb to my assigned floor. Even though my brain was threatening to shut down if I threw in anything more for processing, my thoughts circled back to Colonel Clark again.

He'd really never married? No kids? I couldn't help but wonder if he'd just never met "the one," or if he'd been held back by his seventeen-year-old grief.

Not that I had any idea what his life was like. I couldn't even stand to imagine what I'd do if something happened to my mom, so who was I to judge anyone else? And maybe it was even harder to bear as an adult, when you had a better awareness of what you'd lost. I mean, even though my mom held up the permanent light of optimism, it wasn't like she'd ever moved on and remarried.

I reached the top step, but before I pushed open the door to the next stage of my life, I issued a self-reprieve. *Let it go for tonight, at least.*

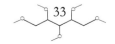

I almost jumped when I stepped through the door into the hallway and found Janet seated just inside. *Has she been waiting for me?* I thought, suddenly realizing that I didn't even know if there was a curfew around here. But I couldn't be late, when there were still all those other kids outside.

Janet quickly closed *Slaughterhouse Five* – in my opinion, one of the most painful books on any high school reading list, but for some reason all the agency people seemed to get into it – and greeted me with a smile.

"Hey, Clio," she said. "That's you." She gestured to the door directly across from where she was sitting – the first door on the right. "After dinner they gave out keys and room assignments; you missed it."

"I was in Colonel Clark's office," I told her, hoping she wouldn't make me elaborate.

"Hmm." She frowned, then probed as expected, "What for?"

"He knew my dad so he wanted to introduce himself." I kept it simple, seeing no need to embarrass any of us with the details. "He told me to come to him if I needed anything."

"Funny," she mused, "that's actually why I'm here. Remember how I told you the staff members were going to act as 'guides' for all of you? Well, you lucked out and got my wing here in the dorm. I am now officially your go-to gal, so if anything comes up, you call on me first, okay?"

She held out my room key and I took it, nodding with relief. "Good – I think it'll be easier to talk to you than the colonel."

"Of course it will." She grinned back conspiratorially, the way I imagined a big sister would. "I'm right across the hall here," she said, hitching back with her thumb. "I got the room closest to the exit to make sure none of you young ladies try to sneak out to visit any young gentlemen during the night."

"Don't worry; I'm way too tired for that," I assured her, and she squeezed my shoulder before retreating into her room with her chair and book.

She tossed one last reminder over her shoulder, "Make sure you call home tonight and let your mom know you're okay." I promised I would, then let myself into my room before I crashed right there on the hallway floor.

FOUR

I was so relieved to finally be in my room that I almost forgot to be jarred by the fact that it was *my room*, as in an exact replica of my room at home. They'd told us this would be a home away from home, even joked that it'd be even better since all of our things would come with us except for annoying siblings, but I still wasn't prepared for the exactness of the replication.

Some extreme makeover team must've worked twenty-four-seven to pack, move, and put back together not just mine, but close to one hundred rooms from around the country. Really, even then, there was no way they could've gotten it all done so fast unless they'd had significantly more lead time than the handful of days they'd given us.

Well, obviously they had more time than us, I rationalized. Besides setting up the facility, they'd had to coordinate telling all of us and getting us here, too. And, to be fair, not calling us the instant they'd unearthed the seventeen-year-old secret had probably been the right thing to do, like not passing on a juicy piece of gossip before verifying the source. But my feelings flipped back and forth. I knew it made sense that the Army'd tried to uncover as much of the truth as they possibly could before approaching us with half-information and guesses, but part of me still felt like they should've told us first, then done their digging while we got used to the idea. Then again, maybe it only sounded so simple now that I'd already somewhat adjusted and also knew that they knew essentially nothing.

I decided to leave that mental discussion for now and focus on the matters at hand, beginning with the ice-blue and gold embroidered comforter and pillows that I'd found perfectly elegant but not old-fashioned when I'd asked for them last Christmas. I saw that my walls were also the same lickable caramel that I painted them every time we moved because, according to my mom, Feng Shui dictated that bedroom walls be some shade of skin to promote harmony.

Not necessarily your own skin color, I could almost hear her quoting the decorating guide, *but somebody's. Certainly not blue or purple or anything disruptive to your subconscious.* And she'd been right, because in each new location I did always find comfort in my private cocoon space.

I tugged on the handle of my grandmother's old

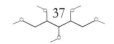

mahogany armoire to reveal my summer shirts folded and stacked in the rainbow-order system I preferred. I couldn't believe my mom had let a van of military movers haul away the irreplaceable family heirloom, but it seemed to've survived the trip alright.

The one thing in the room surely not mine was the black plastic monstrosity on the side of my roll-top desk. I had to do a double-take to confirm that yes, indeed, it was a retro dial-up phone, complete with fat, curly cord. Its square red light blinked at me like an alien eye and, although my first instinct was to toss a sweatshirt over it and make it disappear, I walked over and lifted the chunky handle.

When my ear was greeted with nothing but dead air, I pressed the flashing button – the only thing I could think to do. The robotic response was immediate: *You have one new message.* The recording was not so different from my voice mail, except that the entire message was delivered in the same stunted automation: *You have received a call from…*click, pause, click…"It's Mom, honey." *To return this call, press nine.*

I replaced the receiver, thinking, *Why use this when that funky cord probably won't even reach the bed?* Instead, I pulled out my cell and sprawled across the bed, settling in for a good, long retelling of the day.

I hit the talk button twice to redial the last number – mom's from when I'd called from Newark to let her know that

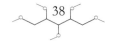

my flight had landed safely and we were about to start the drive north. I waited out a minute of silence, but no ringing. I pulled back to check the screen and sure enough, no bars. I knew we were in the woods but how isolated could we really be in New Jersey? Frustrated, I went back to the black beast and tried to fold my legs as comfortably as possible underneath me on the wooden desk chair.

This time my call out was met with, "Hello, my darling daughter." My mom's voice warmed me through like a Ghirardelli cocoa transfusion. I knew pet names embarrassed some kids, but she called me "love" more often than my own name, and now I curled into the word as if it were a hug.

"Mom, I am so happy to talk to you. Today has been ridiculously long! This is my first brain-break," I told her, realizing that this was really my first chance to process the crazy day, too.

"Baby, I've been thinking about you all day and I'm so glad to hear your voice. Tell me everything that's going on." Unlike most moms, her inquiry was more like that of a girlfriend than a nosy parent.

Knowing she'd want to visualize my end of the line, I started by describing my room, taking it in more fully this time, then worked my way out across the courtyard to the main hall. I knew that the campus wasn't huge, but wasn't sure what else was

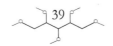

out there and when I'd get to check it out for myself.

"How many kids are there?" she asked.

"Almost a hundred, like they said, so I guess everybody came. And it's like two-thirds girls," I added, and an afterthought slid across my mind: *But there is this one boy…*.

"So many," she whispered, her voice barely audible. "How could none of us have suspected anything?"

Not again, I groaned inwardly. The worst part of this whole situation so far – worse than worrying about having green blood or three stomachs, even – was enduring her constant guilt. It somehow made me feel guilty, and I hadn't even done anything wrong.

"Mom, we've been over this a million times," I reminded her. "You couldn't have known, since I'm totally normal, right?" Being firm but gentle was usually the way to bring her out of it.

"I'm just missing you, sweetheart. It's hard to let go," she added, "like waiting out your first sleepover all over again."

"Oh, right – the one where you dug some night-vision goggles out of Dad's old gear and paid the guy next door to watch the house I was staying at? I wouldn't call that letting go." It was pretty funny in retrospect, although it hadn't been to the mortified eleven-year-old me.

"Because worrying about my daughter is a crime," she retorted, and I could hear the eye roll in her voice. "So back to

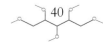

the present – tell me what happened today."

Weirdly enough, the first thing that popped into my mind – for the second time – was Jack. I smiled at the thought of him, but forced myself to tell her about the day that'd begun several long hours before he'd materialized. After an almost twenty-minute-long play-by-play that included Janet, dinner, and Bliss and company as highlights, I got to the part about meeting Colonel Clark.

"Yes, I do know Randall," my mom answered thoughtfully. "He sends a note every year at Christmas to keep in touch. You've probably never noticed it mixed in with all the other cards. He's a very kind man, really took your father's death hard. Harder than I'd expected, actually, since I didn't know him all that well, but they were all like brothers in that unit."

The last thing I wanted was to make her feel sad about my dad tonight when she was already missing me, so I breezed forward. "Anyway, I don't want to keep you up all night – I'm sure I'll have another long day tomorrow and you've got an early flight." She was leaving for California in the morning to promote the upcoming release of the latest book in her *Everlasting Love* series. The timing couldn't have been better, as her agent would keep her constantly busy and I wouldn't have to worry about her being alone.

"Wait," she interjected, "I need one round meta-me

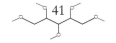

before you go." This was a reference to a game we'd played for as long as I could remember; when she'd hit a block in her writing, she'd give me a word or phrase relevant to the scene she was stuck on, and I'd come back with a hopefully useful metaphor that would spark something to get her back on track. She said that even as a small child I could always give her a fresh outlook, but now my more extensive seventeen-year-old vocab actually made its way into print sometimes. Having a mom who involved me in her work and even used some of my ideas was definitely pretty cool.

"Go," I prompted, and she threw out, "Hot and steamy."

"Geyser," I lobbed back reflexively, causing her to giggle like a teenager. "Clio, I write romance, remember? Not erotica. I'm going for more *sultry*, like a southern summer night."

"Oh." I paused and searched my mind again, but this time hit a wall. "Sorry, Mom, I'm coming up blank. This day has just been way too long." I must be even more wiped than I thought, because I was never this unimaginative.

"Go get some sleep, honey," she said sympathetically. "It's not important. You've got some busy days ahead of you and you need your rest. Call me when you can."

I was already stripping off my clothes to get ready for bed. "Thanks, Mom. Don't forget I've got the neighbors watching you while I'm gone, so no wild parties." We shared a

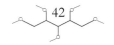

laugh and "I love yous" before hanging up.

Pulling on my tank-top and boxer pajamas, I glanced at my short stack of paperbacks and realized that I was too tired to read even one chapter before lights out. I dropped back onto my pillow, planning to at least think over the day one more time, but my memory didn't get past boarding the plane with Lieutenant Graham before I fell into a deep, dreamless sleep.

FIVE

*T*hursday morning, day two of the great chromosome exploration, had me rushing to what I imagined would be only the first in a series of mandatory lectures.

I blew into the main hall to find that the tables from yesterday had all been cleared out and the chairs rearranged into eight long, forward-facing rows. The rows were split down the middle with six chairs on each side, leaving a center aisle for – no joke – a projector on a table in the back like I hadn't seen since second grade.

It's probably the same one from my second grade class, I thought, *since how many of those dinosaurs still even exist in the world?*

Of course, the back half of the room had filled up first, so I aimed for the open aisle seat capping the fourth row. I saw that, out of habit, we were all jockeying for a position that would allow for unimpeded escape, but I had a feeling no one was going to

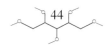

duck out early on our first opportunity for real answers. My butt was a hair away from claiming the prime seat when I got hip-checked down the row by – *who else?* – Garrett.

"Keep it moving, keep it moving," he directed, nudging me down the row, followed by the rest of what was apparently becoming his entourage – Jack, Bliss, and, still as huffy as yesterday but surprisingly sticking with us, Miranda.

"You missed breakfast," Bliss leaned around the guys to tell me, in case I didn't know.

"Yeah, I'm not really a morning person," I admitted, cringing at how fresh and perky the rest of them looked. Granted, a nine a.m. session should have given me plenty of time to fluff-up respectably, too, but I was also willing to bet that having time to hit the Starbucks kiosk outside the dining hall had given them a solid leg up on me. I'd been happy to see that at least if this place wasn't built hi-tech, they still offered some hi-test caffeine. And then hugely disappointed that I'd had to run right by.

"You didn't miss much," Miranda said under her breath, but she was still audible from four chairs away. "No soy milk, no flax seeds, and I doubt the fruit salad was even organic."

Garrett took the opening to offer me a handful of Lucky Charms, saying, "Don't worry; I got your back."

Actually, my favorite cereal, but the hand bowl? Not so much.

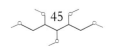

45

"Are you gonna blow me some milk out of your nose, too?" I asked, raising one eyebrow.

He threw his head back and downed the whole handful, then answered through the full-mouth crunch, "Nah, it was really all for me – your loss."

"You are such a freak," I laughed, shaking my head because he was exactly the kind of friend I needed to jolt my brain out of over-thinking mode.

"The Starbucks is open all day; you can get up to speed after this," Jack chimed in, seemingly reading my mind.

"Thanks," I responded lamely, then scrambled for any kind of decent follow-up.

I lost my chance when Colonel Clark stepped up to the podium, backed by a stocky, crew-cut-sporting guy in a lab coat and a toffee-skinned, model-gorgeous woman in a red tailored suit. I laughed to myself at how the colonel's blue button-down completed the trifecta of patriotic colors and wondered if they'd planned it.

"I'll go with you," Bliss whispered one last line at the same moment Randall held up a hand signaling he was about to begin.

"Good morning, everyone," he called cheerfully. "I hope you fueled up with a smart breakfast and are ready to take in some good information." The groans in the audience indicated

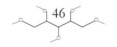

that nobody was really up for class today, so he was quick to reassure us. "Don't worry; you're not in summer school. I already told Dr. Larson that if anyone falls asleep, he's fired." He paused and grinned, trying so hard that I almost felt bad for him. "Seriously, kids," he went on, "he's here to fill you all in on what we know about the C9x project, and he is going to try to stay the line between boring you to tears and insulting your intelligence by dumbing things down. There will be a brief overview, followed by the opportunity to ask questions, so let's get started." I guessed he'd be introducing the woman later, since she hadn't moved.

Dr. Larson stepped up to the speaking spot, keeping both hands in his pockets to show he had no need for notes. Or normal communicative gestures. Not a great sign.

A diagram of something science-y appeared on the drop-down screen behind him, but I had no idea what I was supposed to be seeing, so I focused on listening. "Chromosome nine is an actively studied but largely unmapped chromosome spanning approximately 145 million base pairs of nucleic acid – the building blocks of DNA," he delivered in one long breath.

Okay, I figured out pretty quickly, *I guess he's diving straight into biology.* Hopefully there'd be a handout later because this was looking kind of rough out of the gate.

He continued lecturing, "During in-utero development,

chromosomes may appear to break and then rejoin, most often occurring in a non-coding sequence and therefore not resulting in any type of mutation. Those DNA-level breaks happen relatively frequently, and the DNA simply repairs itself." Though this seemed to me a natural point to pause, maybe make some eye contact, he stayed stock still in his delivery.

"However," he went on, "wrong re-joining of a gene can spur activity at a critical time and produce a hybrid gene. Still, even these rearranged chromosomes are most often what is called 'cell-lethal' and are quickly removed from the cell population. What we want to make sure did not happen to any of you is that those rearranged chromosomes were able to survive and transmit, becoming derivative chromosomes." He finally paused and scanned the crowd to make sure we were all still with him. It was dry, but I was managing to keep up, anxious to hear what kind of crank messages may be coursing through my genes. I should've known I'd be let down.

"Unfortunately, with no lab documentation, we have to begin at square one in trying to determine which of the twelve hundred or so genes of chromosome nine were targeted and what mutations may have occurred due to possible complications like inversion, deletion, or translocation during the rejoining process I described before. We're hoping to be able to then use that genetic data to work backward until we can eventually re-create the drug

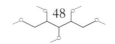

48

that was administered."

I had to award him points for semi-speediness since it was now clear that he didn't plan to go on all day, but I wasn't thrilled that I didn't really know much more now than I did before. And Larson was definitely finished, because Randall-to-the-Rescue reclaimed the microphone and offered, "We're ready to respond to any questions you may have."

A hand shot up from somewhere close behind me and Colonel Clark nodded in acknowledgement of the speaker.

"It sounds like this study could take years. I thought we were only supposed to be here for a couple weeks." The complaint came from a tall, athletic guy who clearly did not want to cool his heels here indefinitely.

Randall fielded this one himself. "Don't worry, folks," he began, and I couldn't help thinking, *We're in high school; our lives are nothing* but *worries.* "You'll only be here for the agreed-upon term," he explained quickly. "We'll gather as much data as we can during that period and then, after you've returned home, our work will continue for as long as it takes to get the answers we need."

Another hand went up; another nod gave permission to speak.

"So, we just go home like nothing even happened? And maybe five years from now we get a call that we have some weird

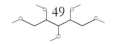

disease?" This concern came from a striking brunette who found it clearly disturbing that she could end up "weird."

"I'll answer that." The up-until-now quiet woman on the stage stepped forward to address us. "Chances are, you will spend the rest of your lives as you are today – perfectly healthy and normal." I instantly found her voice too cool to be comforting, though that was clearly not her intent. I guessed that it must be her job to smooth over sticky situations, but her words felt as gritty as sandpaper to me.

"The dozen or so known syndromes related to chromosome nine usually also negatively affect one's outward appearance," she continued. "Judging by the fact that you're all quite attractive people, it's most probable that we'll actually find nothing of any significance at all." She finished with a glittering, almost pageant-ready smile that closed the last tiny part of my mind that I'd tried to keep open to her.

Experience told me that when someone tells you not to worry, it's because they're already doing it enough for both of you. Though I wanted her words to be true, it seemed to me that if they were, we wouldn't have all needed to be secretly delivered to this government facility. For the first time, the possibility of a real problem sank like a stone in my gut. *I knew I should've eaten breakfast*, I thought, *just like I always need that first funnel cake to hold things down before riding a roller coaster.*

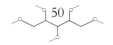

I peered around a nodding-off Garrett to look at Jack, who remained politely quiet but bore a skeptical crease at the side of his mouth that felt like the mate to mine. Beyond him, I saw Bliss looking a bit frightened. Just as I opened my mouth to reassure her, the woman up front decided to wrap things up anyway.

"That's all we have time for this morning so let's go ahead and break now," she said with finality, though I thought there were still a few half-raised hands waiting with unanswered questions. "Everyone will reconvene this afternoon with their assigned groups."

"Ah," Garrett stretched his arms so far over his head that his shirt pulled out of his waistband, revealing the bottom two cans of the six-pack that I was pretty sure he showed off proudly and often. "I feel like I need a nap after that," he yawned.

"Besides the one you took *during* that?" I teased, surprised at how easily I could talk with such a cute guy that I barely knew – two things that normally cemented my mouth shut.

"Yeah, that was all the same stuff as the press page on the web," Jack chimed in. "I didn't get anything new, except maybe a charley horse." He confirmed the source of his complaint by reaching down to rub his calf.

My eyes followed the line of his leg, the lean muscle capturing my attention in a way that even Garrett's fab abs hadn't

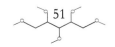

been able to. Before I got caught staring, I turned my attention to Bliss. "Still up for Starbucks?"

"Absolutely," she agreed, popping out of her seat. "I need to get out of this room and get some air after that creepfest."

"It's just the military training," Miranda said dismissively. "Nobody teaches them how to relax and be normal."

"No worries, hot pants – it's all good," Garrett added, probably the one kid here who'd never had an actual worry.

"How can you be so relaxed?" Bliss countered, obviously the yin to his yang.

"So long as they only want to watch me play ball and prick my finger once in awhile, I'm cool with that. We'll do our time, show what we've got, then we're outta here," Garrett shared his simple take on it.

Fortunately, Jack's words did a better job of calming her. "He's right. Don't panic until you have a good reason to or you'll make yourself nuts."

I was briefly tempted to throw out a panic attack of my own to get my share of his valiant reassurance, but I knew I could never believably pull off the damsel-in-distress bit.

"Come on, Bliss," I led her away by the elbow before she could absorb any more of Jack's highly coveted – by me – attention, and tossed what I hope was a casual nod to the boys, saying, "Later, guys." And I wondered if it was just my

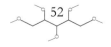

imagination, or if Jack looked a little disappointed to see me go.

SIX

*B*ack in the lobby, Bliss waited in line with me for my mocha latte – the sole vice of my mother's that she repeatedly kicked herself for passing on to me. I found it hilarious that my mom actually worried about my growth being stunted when I already stood almost five-foot-six. Plus, like my mom, I only indulged on rough mornings where I'd overslept and needed to get up to speed ASAP for something important – two things that thankfully didn't collide very often in my regular life.

When my order came up, I patted my pockets only to realize that I didn't have a purse or any money on me. As soon as Bliss figured out what I was doing, she was quick to fill me in. "It's all free, like the meals. No expenses spared to keep us comfy at Camp C9x, remember?"

Huh, I thought. I might not be in such a hurry to bail in a couple of weeks, after all – this was turning out to be the kind of

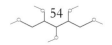

place I could hang out for the whole summer.

Bliss picked up a ginormous egg salad sandwich from the display case as I snagged a chicken wrap for myself and we headed outside.

We claimed the sunniest – and last available – courtyard bench and breathed in the beautiful day. Although it was almost noon, there was nothing like the stifling heat we were both used to in the South and, unlike the majority of other kids who'd parked in the shade, I could've bathed in the rays all day.

Bliss had her sandwich open first and an explanation to go with it. "I never get to eat like this at home. This is my kind of salad – hold the lettuce, double the mayo. If my mom knew we were headed to a food free-for-all, she probably would've air-dropped a crate of MREs."

"Meals Ready to Eat?" I asked, not entirely sure I'd gotten it right. At least I knew some of the basic terms; hopefully enough to fit in.

"Oh, I forget you're not a service kid. I'll try to go light on the acronyms. How do you know any Army stuff at all, after missing out on our glamorous lifestyle?" She hardly got all the words out before inhaling another giant mouthful.

"We still go on base a lot," I explained, "you know, for the doctor, dentist, that stuff. Right now we use the Navy base since it's closest to the city, but they're all the same, right?"

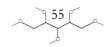

Bliss scooted away from me down the bench. "Don't want to be too close when the lightning strikes you for that," she warned.

"Ooh, my mistake," I replied, teasing, and hoping she was, too. "Don't we all play for the same team?" I asked, hoping she wasn't serious.

"Just don't say that kind of stuff in front of my mom," she said, wagging one pinkie finger at me as she spoke so as not to lose her grip on the mayo monstrosity. "She'll learn you a good lesson on branch rivalries, for sure."

"So your mom's pretty hard-core, huh?" A worried frown crossed her sun-kissed face at my question, but she shooed it away just as quickly as it'd appeared.

"I'm guessing you're the only one here who doesn't know who my legendary mother is." It was a question and a statement rolled into one.

"Should I?" I hoped it was okay to ask, that there wasn't some wild scandal involved.

"Probably not, unless you read a lot of old-man news mags," she answered, before clearing her throat and announcing as if reading a headline, "Paula Campbell, Two-Star Major General, Appointed to United States Army South, Fort Sam Houston. First Woman to Assume Coveted Post."

"Wow," I said. "That's impressive." Although her

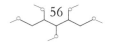

daughter didn't seem all that impressed.

"Yeah, well, it's like half the time I'm the news story. *She's famous but everyone always wants to know what I'm doing* – I hate it. She's always on top of me to put on a good show." She mimicked, "*They can't deny I manage both a successful career and take care of my family when they see how perfect my daughter is.*" The quote didn't come off much like a motherly compliment.

I wanted to say something more sympathetic than "that sucks," but I also didn't know Bliss well enough yet to know her bounds. I finally went with, "Is that why she named you Bliss?"

"No, that was my dad," she said, her expression softening. "We were stationed at Fort Bliss when I was born, near where he grew up in New Mexico. He thought it was the best place on Earth and he said that with my mom working so hard and gone half the time that it took forever to get pregnant. So when I was born, his life was complete. My mom thought it was hokey, that I'd end up as a hairdresser because no one would ever take me seriously with that name, but my dad insisted. Since he was the one who stayed home to take care of me, he won."

"Sounds like he'd get along great with my mom – two goofy romantics," I empathized.

"Maybe she can send him an autographed book," she suggested, and we laughed our way out of the heavy part of the conversation just in time for a drop-in guest.

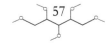

"Get me one, too," Miranda said as she entered stage left. "Not that I've ever read her stuff, but I will if she's got some spicy scenes." *Ugh.* Her abrasiveness was one thing, but if she turned out to be slutty, too, our friendship would be short-lived.

"So are the books hot?" she pursued, undeterred by the lack of invitation.

I tried to stay main-line, but it still came out snippy when I said, "The first *ew* is because the hero, Rex, is modeled after my dad." My hopeless-romantic mom was a firm believer in soul mates and still thought of my dad as her one and only, even though he'd been gone for sixteen years. And secretly, I found it actually kind of sweet, not delusional.

"So your mom is Wendy Hart?" It seemed Miranda did know the series, after all.

"Actually, my mom is Regina Kaid, but, yes, her pen name is Wendy Hart."

"Niiice," she purred approvingly. "Dadd-o really must know his way around the romper room the way your mom writes about it."

"Second *ew*," I went on as if she hadn't interjected, "is for talking about your sex life, which is definitely TMI." Bliss nodded in shared discomfort.

Miranda exchanged her smug look for an appalled one. "Do you two not listen to me at all? *This*," she drew out the

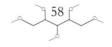

word, while making a sweeping gesture to indicate her flawless figure, "is a temple, ladies. Tem-ple. Boys may worship at my feet, but that's as far as the masses get."

I knew my grandmother would've admonished, *Close the trap, you're not catching flies*, when my mouth dropped open, but it was an involuntary reaction.

Miranda must have misread my shock at her abstinence as embarrassment over my own – in actuality, nonexistent – sex life, because she launched into a lecture. "Please do not tell me you are dumb enough to put out! You know the free-milk-and-cow thing is totally true." Her last words made Bliss giggle, which in turn infected me.

"Obviously my benevolent wisdom is wasted on you two," Miranda huffed, crossing her arms over her chest, but not making any real move to leave.

"No, we totally appreciate your concern," I tried to recover, but couldn't fully get my laughter under control. And Bliss was now so hopelessly lost in her giggling that I prepared myself to dodge any egg chunks that might launch out of her nose.

"This is why I shouldn't bother talking to people." I could tell by Miranda's tone that we were almost dismissed. "I just stopped to tell you that they posted the afternoon sessions and we're all in the same group," she said flatly. "We're supposed

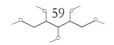

59

to meet in the clearing, essentially right now."

Right now? I glanced at my watch and was startled to see how long we'd been sitting there. I was pretty sure I'd never talked so long – and so easily – with a brand-new friend. And thinking about how much I liked Bliss also made me feel a little bit bad for Miranda, who did seem to be trying in her own way. Just because her nice kitty was more like anybody else's rabid jaguar didn't make her a bad person – she just kept her good side pushed way, *way* down deep.

"Thanks for the heads up," I told her earnestly. "We'll go with you."

Bliss sent me a wide-eyed message behind Miranda's back that clearly said, *Same group? Fuuun-tastic.*

I offered a shrug in return to answer, *How bad can it be?* I guessed we'd find out soon enough.

SEVEN

As we got closer, I was surprised to find at least half the kids on campus descending on the designated meeting area; apparently, they hadn't just divided us into same-sized groups like I'd assumed they would. I found myself casually searching the crowd for Jack's tousled hair, but, disappointingly, saw no sign of him.

"He's not here," Bliss said quietly in my left ear.

"What? Who?" I knew my confused act was probably not at all believable, but I didn't want to admit my growing crush was so easy to spot.

"Jack's at the gym with Garrett; they were talking about it at breakfast while you were busy *sleeping.*" She emphasized the last word to soften the blow.

"Oh." My tiny response was no reflection of how crushed I felt — ridiculously so, considering that I hardly knew him.

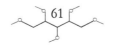

Thankfully, Bliss, who I was fast-track getting to know – and love – wasn't looking to call me out about him. And at least without him here, I had a shot at actually paying attention like I was supposed to.

Everyone was assembling under a huge, open-air tent like I'd expect to see at a wedding reception, except that instead of a traditional white canopy, this one was covered with the green and brown blobs of camouflage. *Are they trying to hide us from photographers in low-flying planes or something?* I couldn't imagine why the media would even bother to track us down when there was nothing to report on.

Somebody better get this show on the road, I thought, trying to rein in my overactive imagination before I rode any further into conspiracy territory. Too much free time for me always led to crazy over-thinking, and this setting gave me way too much material to work with.

I shouldn't have worried, since Miranda wasn't about to leave me to my own thoughts for long. "I don't see why the artsies got the main hall," she complained. "There's only nine of them; they should've just stuck them in a hallway somewhere."

"I actually like being outside," I argued, fully opposed to being stuck inside all afternoon. "Give it a chance." Before she could retaliate with a tirade against pollen exposure or some other nonsense, we were called to order.

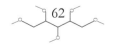

"Hello? Hello!" A voice called from the front, and I moved to look over and between the heads of the other kids until I finally saw Janet. Everyone shushed just as she mumbled, "They should've gotten me a bullhorn," making the aside actually more audible than her previous calls for attention.

Once all heads had turned in her direction and appeared to be listening, she brightened and launched into her welcoming speech.

"Campers!" she called, and the crowd responded with a unanimous groan.

"Class?" Her hesitant second salutation was met with more muttering.

"Guys and Gals. Beautiful People." Now that she had us, she pushed forward. "Welcome to your first group exploration." This statement got no reaction from the group, due to our collective uncertainty, but Janet wasn't about to let that stop her hard-won roll. "Based on yesterday's interviews," she said, "we put everyone into like-groups. There are two other sections convening right now as well – one of the very athletic kids, the other the very artistic or musical ones."

"What're we – leftovers? A whole lot of nothing special?" someone grumbled loudly enough for us all to hear, but not distinctly enough for me to pinpoint the speaker.

"Of course not! I think of you as more of the 'general

population.' Based on sheer numbers, you're the group that most represents the true result of C9x. The others are more…divergent," she said diplomatically, adding, "which makes you our most valuable subjects."

I, for one, wasn't about to complain; the last thing I wanted was to diverge any further from normal. And I guessed by the resounding quiet that most of the others were feeling the same way.

"Well, let's get to work!" Janet clapped her hands together, signaling it was time for whatever activity she'd planned for us. "We're going to try a little exercise today based on what many of you talked about during processing – how you think something like, *Don't see me*, and then sometimes feel like it worked, that you'd somehow faded from sight. Does that make sense – something you can try to show me?"

The exercise sounded simple enough, but it was the other part of what she'd said that tumbled around in my brain like shoes in a dryer – the "many" part. *Other kids had told her they did that, too? Not just me?* I wasn't sure if I should be excited that there were others like me, or upset that now even my thoughts weren't my own.

"Each of you needs your own space." Janet broke into my thoughts, at the same time taking hold of my upper arms and sliding me a couple of feet away from Bliss. When she next moved Miranda a few feet further down from her, the others started to see the emerging pattern and began to arrange themselves. If anyone else's mind was flailing like mine, they gave no sign of it, so I shook my head clear to at least look like I had it together.

"Make sure to leave room for me to walk between you, so I can get to everybody," Janet shouted over the shuffling bodies, then added under her breath, "How'd I draw the short straw to direct the cast of thousands?" It seemed obvious to me why they'd assigned her to the largest group; she was the easiest officer to be around – that I'd met, anyway – and we liked her enough to actually pay attention.

I waited for some kind of order to begin, but saw that Janet was already waiting, watching us expectantly. For what, I wasn't exactly sure, but it looked like self-starting time.

I settled into position, shifting my weight a little into my left hip to get comfortable, and tried to find something to focus my eyes on. *That blue jay perched in the shortest pine? Uh-uh.* It'd probably fly off any second and break my concentration. Next I considered the girl in the capri pants right in front of me, standing primly with one ankle crossed over the other. Then I dismissed her, too; she was totally primed to lose her balance and, with my luck, I'd fall over just watching her go down. Process of elimination left me with only one sensible option; I closed my

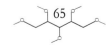

eyes and tried to wipe out all distractions.

I began silently repeating the suggested mantra, *You can't see me; I'm not even here.* After a moment, I felt exactly what I'd expected to – nothing. Not lighter, not tingly, and not invisible to murderers. *Did Janet forget the part about how this only worked in dreams?* I wondered. Because I was pretty sure that was the key to disappearing – being in the non-reality dimension. But I knew I might as well keep trying, since there really was no other choice. I doubted if I quit, they'd let me go take a nap or something.

I felt like I was trying just as hard to not think about how it was going for everyone else as I was focusing on disappearing, but I managed to keep up the mental chant. Doing both took so much concentration that Janet actually startled me when she called a stop on time from somewhere not far off to my left.

I opened my eyes, feeling somewhat disoriented, like I'd just woken up. *Apparently repeating the same thing for long enough can lull you into a sort of trance*, I figured. Luckily, the canopy was there to block the direct sunlight, because my eyes needed a minute to readjust from the darkness behind my lids.

The rustling of the others made me suddenly aware of how intense the silence had been before. Had I closed out all the surrounding noise, or had everyone been that incredibly still? Maybe both.

I turned to Bliss, who met my eyes with a weak smile and

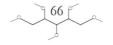

a scrunched forehead as if to say, *You? Anything? Nothing here.*

I shrugged back to signal no excitement on my end either, unsure if we were allowed to talk yet or were supposed to wait for further instructions.

"Great job, guys," Janet called to unfreeze us as she worked her way back to the front. I knew she'd told us she'd be weaving her way in and out of the rows, but either she hadn't checked up on me, or I'd been really out of it, because I hadn't heard a whisper of a step from her.

"I know that was a long time to stay still," she apologized, "so I'm just going to call it a day and let you go."

A long time? I felt sure it'd only been a couple of minutes, but a peek at my watch indicated that it had, in fact, been more than twenty. No wonder people were complaining about cramped muscles. My joints cracked as I stretched them out, and I decided that if we did this again, next time I was sitting down for it.

"Same time, same location tomorrow," Janet called out over the disbursement, confirming my thought.

Not sure what else to do, I started to follow in the same direction Bliss and Miranda and the others were heading. It looked like everyone had the same idea: *Get moving before she figures out we didn't actually do anything and calls us back.*

But I'd only taken a few steps when Janet caught me by

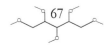

the arm and asked, "How do you feel?"

Like the weakest member of the herd, I thought, *since I'm always getting snagged by the adults here.*

My audible response was, "Disappointed, I guess, that nothing happened." I left off that I could've told her so ahead of time, not sure that was what she wanted to hear right now.

"So you didn't feel anything?" She tempered her own disappointment so that it came off more like curiosity.

She'd said on the first day that all they expected from us was the truth, so I gave it to her. "Surprised that so much time had passed," I answered, shrugging.

"Hey, don't sweat it; tomorrow's another day. Got to go to staff review and make my report," she said, her glance flickering toward a tiny camera I hadn't noticed before, mounted where the post met the canvas at the corner of the tent. Now that I knew what to look for, I picked out all six of them.

I turned back to ask her what they were for, but she was already making tracks in the other direction. I hurried to catch up with the others, wondering if the other groups had anything better to report.

EIGHT

*I*t turned out nobody had anything exciting to share at all – nobody I knew, anyway. Of course, I was kind of limited to my one and a half new friends that were in the same group as me, and the two guys who I hadn't seen since their sessions.

I didn't even know if Jack and Garrett were in the same group. Janet'd said the rest of the kids were split into jocks and indies; I didn't have trouble figuring out which one Garrett fell into, but Jack was a bit of a mystery. He clearly had the hand-eye coordination to play sports, but all that muse talk made me think there was an artisty soul in there, too. I hoped I'd get a chance to find out.

I powered through Friday alongside Bliss and Miranda, finding it as exhausting as the two previous days. Not that the second full day of group sessions had been any more challenging than the first, but the long periods of intense concentration were starting to wear me down. The staff must've sensed the give-upness building in us, because they'd kindly blocked the weekend off as free time.

When I finally woke up on Saturday with a lazy stretch, I reveled in the luxury of not having to rush anywhere. Unfortunately, my mind had only two speeds – on or off, no slow. Before I could even open my eyes, I was already revisiting the conclusion Bliss, Miranda, and I were all starting to come to – that this whole invisibility idea was kind of hokey.

None of us had experienced anything but boredom and irritation. With the only activity being stand still and focus on impossible thoughts, fun camp was quickly becoming not-so-much.

The three of us agreed that, for Monday's session, we needed to make a point of being in the back instead of our usual front to get a new perspective. That way we could scope out the other kids and see how everyone else was doing without having to approach and interrogate a bunch of people we didn't really know.

And, to be fair, there had been one other activity besides "work." Almost as if someone decided it was time for some forced bonding, last night had been our first "fun" event. Janet invited our whole floor to her room for movie night, which not only turned out to be not as lame as I'd predicted, but actually

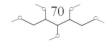

such a good time that we'd hung out there until almost one in the morning.

She'd produced her favorite romantic comedy, *Pretty Woman*, and, although we'd conceded that Richard Gere was decent enough for an older guy, we'd countered by introducing her to the boys of *New Moon*. Thinking back, I had to laugh out loud at the memory of Bliss's doll-perfect face contorted – *Arooo!* – into a werewolf howl.

Yeah, day three'd sure had her busting out of her shell. So the running tally was: day one – no score, the awkward meeting with Clark cancelling the fun of dinner; day two – negative points for both the boring seminar and the useless first group session. Movie night had been good enough to offset the tedious group sessions of day three, and lunch with Jack between the two had been a super bonus. Okay, Bliss, Miranda, Garrett, and another jock he'd been working out with had been there, too, but that wasn't important.

And I'd finally learned that even though Jack was hanging out with the jocks for practice, he wasn't really feeling it and was thinking of switching groups to see if there was a better fit. I had no such issue, having not one athletic, musical, or artistic bone, organ, or tissue in my entire body, but I could see how it would be difficult for him. In just the little time we'd spent together, I'd already seen a million different and interesting sides to Jack.

Unfortunately, his curling grin shorted out all the connections between my brain and my mouth, so I hadn't been able to ask many of the clever questions I'd thought up.

Maybe it'd be better if he stayed away from my practice group, I thought wryly, *at least until I get my hands on some anti-idiot pills.*

Sighing, I shoved back the covers and looked at the clock on my desk to see that – *yikes!* – it was already noon.

I scrambled the rest of the way out of bed. No group session did not mean no getting ready today – far from it. Last night's mini girl-fest had been like a social rehearsal for the campus-wide main event scheduled for tonight, and I needed to get moving.

First stop – shower, I commanded myself, hoping it'd be empty at this late hour.

When I'd first seen how amazing our rooms were, I'd crossed my fingers that I'd get my own bathroom, too, but I'd found that this dream did have its limits after all. I piled into my arms shampoo, conditioner, soap, puff, pick, and razor and trekked down the carpeted hall, finding not another soul in sight. The quiet was great for getting ready in peace, but after having been late every morning so far, sleeping through lunch today was sure to make me the team slackscot. *At least my hair'll be clean when they put the crown on me*, I teased myself.

I set my stuff on the bench seat outside the shower,

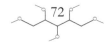

climbed past the curtain, and peeled off my pajamas, draping them over the rod. Thankfully, they'd put in individual stalls to spare us the prison-nightmare of a group shower, not that it seemed to matter with the off-hours I was keeping these days.

I'd also been happy to discover that the bathrooms were spotless. With twelve girls sharing it, I'd been sure the place would be trashed, but, even after four days, there wasn't a hair on the floor or a smudge on any of the mirrors. I hadn't seen anyone actually doing any cleaning, but they weren't making us do it, which had been my worst fear. As far as I could tell, we were only responsible for our own rooms; every afternoon I came back to the same rumpled heap of a bed that I'd left in the morning.

I hummed to myself as I lathered up, not realizing until I was rinsing off that I hadn't brought clean clothes to change into. I briefly considered making the walk in my towel, gambling that the hall would still be deserted, but then decided to put my pajamas back on, just to be safe. Anyone could show up at any time; privacy was definitely not a guarantee at Hotel USGov.

And speak of the devil – not wholly *un*literally – it was a good thing I'd covered up, since I almost crashed into the girl I'd heard called Alexis right outside the bathroom door. It took all of my coordination to juggle my toiletries while standing on one foot so that I could use the other one to hold the door. When she passed through without even looking at me, and even the air around her seemed to push me back, I wished I'd just let it close on her. She hadn't lightened up at all since that first day I'd seen her in the dining hall; she was still as dark and angry as a walking storm cloud.

I made it back to my room and opened my door to find Alexis's polar opposite – sunshiny Bliss – sprawled across my bed with *US Weekly* paged through almost to the end.

"Hey, guess who I just ran into – literally," I vented, almost expecting her to be there. Between group sessions and close room assignments, she was quickly becoming my constant – like a self-assigned buddy. And I'd scored on the pick. We just clicked, in a way that I never had with anyone else, and sometimes it felt like I'd known her my whole life instead of less than a week.

"Please don't say Miranda," she groaned. "I booked it after suffering through the whole lunch with her; there's no way she could've made it back here already. Oh, I brought you back something," she added, and I followed her head tilt to my desk where a tuna salad waited for me in a plastic go-box. "There may be a leafy bed at the bottom, but it wouldn't have been lunch by Bliss without my signature condiment."

I dumped my lotions and potions unceremoniously onto the desk chair and settled cross-legged on the bed facing her. "Thanks," I said before returning to the subject of my bad hall encounter. "No, it was Cruella de Vil dressed in black, black, and blacker, right down to her thigh-high leather Viviennes. Julia would be so skeeved at the blatant style molestation."

"Why is she like that?" Bliss asked with a delicate shudder. "Is she trying to scare people?"

"You know it's all an act," I assured her, then philosophized, "Didn't your mom ever tell you that some people think negative attention is better than no attention at all?"

"No, but I know that less attention is almost as good as no attention," offered my shy friend. "Maybe it's a cry for help. Do you think we should ask her to walk over with us tonight?"

"No way she's going," I said, reminding her, "She couldn't even be bothered to shuffle ten steps down the hall for movies last night."

"True," she admitted. "I think I'd prefer to show up with my head attached instead of leaving it bitten-off in the hallway, anyway. I'm so glad she's not in our group."

Even though Alexis lived on our floor, we lucky "invisibles" rarely saw her since she somehow fell into the arty/music group. I couldn't imagine her having any talents beyond murder and mayhem – which totally had to be the name of her band if she had one – but I was happy for the separation.

"So what're you wearing tonight?" Bliss skipped to a happier subject.

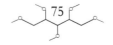

Before I could admit I needed serious help in that department, in barged our third and not-so-gallant musketeer.

"I'm here to offer my expertise in prepping you two for the festivities," Miranda announced, pushing open the door that I thought was supposed to lock automatically behind me. "Consider it my good deed for the day."

"Thanks, but I think we'll be alright." I told her, afraid to be too subtle, or she'd put down roots. I had no intention of setting myself up for the critique I'd have to endure by changing in front of her.

"Well, don't say I didn't offer…," she strung the last sound out, giving us one last chance to beg her to stay.

My brain knew to keep quiet and let her go, but my mouth was running without authorization again. "It's not going to be a major production, you know," I told her. "I'm sure everyone's going to stand around acting like they're too good to be there and probably not even dance, just like at home."

"Good," Bliss chimed in with relief, "because I'm not the best dancer." I had to agree with her. It's not like I was against dancing, but let's just say they'd have to mess with a lot more of my chromosomes to make it my super-ability.

"Unacceptable scenario." My words had backfired, riling Miranda up instead of settling her down. "I fully intend to showcase my cake moves," she declared, "and the rest of you

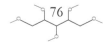
76

could use the cardio."

For once, she actually took note of my reaction and read my sharply cocked eyebrow correctly. "Nothing personal," she covered quickly. "Everyone needs cardiovascular exercise – it's heart-smart." I suspected this backpedaling was a move she reserved for the very few individuals she considered almost friends, so I let her off.

"Well, I'm off to get ready," she chirped. "Holler if you change your minds." With a toodling wave she was gone.

She was barely out the door when Bliss said, "Do you think she'll do her fantabulous fanny-shaking near us, or in a circle of boys?"

I gave her a knowing look and she amended, "Right – rhetorical question. So back to business. Show me your dress for tonight."

"I packed more camp than club. I didn't bring anything dressy." And I hadn't considered that to be a problem until just this minute.

"Hmm." She paused, putting a thoughtful finger to her lips, then jumped up and headed for the door. "I'll be right back."

I unwrapped my towel turban to start combing out my hair while I waited, but she was back halfway through the first brushstroke with a shimmery-sheer light blue sheath.

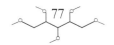

"Perfect," she said, nudging the hanger up under my chin to see the effect.

"Are you serious?" It was an amazing dress, but she couldn't mean for me to wear it. I had to ask, "Aren't you wearing this?"

"No, I'm going with a pink strapless one – my favorite. Besides, this color goes great with your hair."

"Yeah, I'm sure not going to fight you for pink. Or orange or red," I listed the trifecta of colors sure to make my hair look like burnt sweet potatoes.

She'd also peaked my curiosity about her closet. "Did you bring your entire wardrobe?" I asked.

"Pretty much," she confirmed, like it was the norm. "My mom told me to pack everything. She figured we'd do at least one press conference here, if not regular filming. We Campbells have to keep up appearances, you know," she finished with a wink.

"Do you know what a disaster I'd be if you weren't here?" I was almost teary with relief and gratitude as I walked her to the door.

"Yeah – a hungry, naked one," she teased, squeezing my hand in returned affection. "I'll swing by here and pick you up on my way to the *soiree*."

"It's a date!" I called after her as she headed back to her room to change.

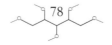

Janet, probably roused by my yelling, opened her door across the hall and poked her head out.

"Sorry," I apologized, immediately feeling guilty for being so loud, especially since it was very unlike me.

"No problem," she said, waving off the disturbance and examining the dress in my hand. "Getting ready for the big dance?"

"Yeah, thanks to Bliss I think it's gonna be a good time," I answered. "Are you going?"

"Do you mean am I *chaperoning*?" Janet teased. "No," she informed me with a laugh, "but I did make the play list."

Doubt must have flickered across my face because she went on the mock-defensive. "Don't worry; I kept it current – nothing more than five years old and nothing too obscure. I'm only ten years older than you, not a hundred, okay?"

"Oh, don't *you* worry," I retorted, matching my light tone to hers. "I'll report back with your score later." I smiled and ducked back into my room. I resumed brushing my long hair smooth with new motivation, having decided that we *were* going to have a good time at this dance and Miranda wasn't even going to have to make us.

And what about Jack? He and Garrett'd both said they'd be there, but I was much more concerned about one than the other. Between the group sessions and the crowded meals, I hadn't had a chance to talk to Jack alone since the flying fruit fiasco, no alliteration intended.

Hopefully tonight I'd get that chance, not that I had any clue what I wanted to say to him. Maybe walking over with Miranda wouldn't be such a bad idea, after all; she never seemed to run out of things to say....

NINE

*T*he pulsating music drew the three of us, Miranda included, across the courtyard to the main building where the great room had supposedly been transformed beyond recognition – we were about to find out. Good thing we didn't have far to travel, because I was getting more nervous with each silver-sandaled step. For the fifth time in as many minutes, Bliss slapped away my hand as it drifted up to tug on one of the loose strands of my tousled updo.

"It was hard work giving you that 'I just threw myself together' look, you know. Do not screw it up." Bliss growled each word of warning, so I obediently laced my fingers together in front of me.

I was glad to see a few other stragglers coming up behind us, making me feel better that we were not the last of the last. A fashionably late entrance was not my thing – it seemed pretty rude to me, making everybody else wait around for you.

Miranda certainly couldn't have cared less about anyone else's agenda when she'd taken her sweet time getting ready – at least half an hour longer than Bliss and I. Since the majority of her prep work had somehow occurred in front of my bedroom mirror, we'd been forced to wait for her. She'd made us examine each of four outfits from every angle as she danced before finally picking a one-shouldered violet top and low-rise fitted black silk pants. When I'd warned her not to bend over too far or risk a panty reveal and she'd informed me that she was, in fact, going commando, I'd decided it was past go-time and dragged her out the door.

Having chosen ballet flats, Bliss stood the tiniest of our group but the most classically beautiful. She'd brushed out her hair into a sheet of spun-gold and stuck with the same makeup palette I had – a light swipe of mascara and lipstick, hers being the same cotton-candy shade as her dress. Her heart-shaped neckline also really flattered her chest, but I kept that to myself instead of embarrassing her into going back and changing.

We reached the propped-open door and before we even stepped inside, I had the sense we were walking onto the set of a bad teen movie. I found it troubling enough that they even *had* decorations – very nineties of them – but *Come on*; a huge banner announced that there was also a *theme*.

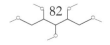

The nicest thing I could say was that you couldn't fault the attention to detail they'd paid in creating "Summer Dreaming." Working from the top down, they'd veiled the entire ceiling with what had to be a thousand light blue balloons, then randomly floated up some oversized white ones, too – clouds in the sky, of course. Having had to turn off all the fluorescent lights, they'd ringed strings upon strings of white lights around the ceiling, emcee table, and scattered two-person tables. The lights I was happy with, unlike the shiny green and blue tinsel they'd draped floor to ceiling on all sides. I assumed it was meant to represent trees blending up into sky but, in reality, I just felt like I was trapped in a pretend carwash.

In keeping with the theme, to our immediate right stretched a long table covered in a grass-green tablecloth edged with faux strawberry vines. And, proving the staff was lacking not only style but also sense, there sat an honest-to-goodness punch bowl – another unnecessarily unearthed fossil – filled with a red mystery drink that no girl in this room was going to let within ten feet of her dress. Rounding out the smorgasbord of no-nos were raw celery and broccoli to stick in the teeth, ranch dip for canine breath, daisy-frosted cupcakes to guarantee crumby, sticky, unholdable hands, and the ultimate outfit-ruiner – salsa with tortilla chips.

So our threesome's obvious first move was a hard left,

away from disaster and into the decent-sized dancing crowd. It looked like they hadn't needed Miranda to start the party after all; Garrett was successfully serving as ringleader, his height making him easy to spot at the heart of the crowd. Because of his tall vantage point, he spied us right away and waved us into his clutch of fans before we could double-back and seek cover.

We began making our way toward him, only to be diverted into a situation bound to be even more embarrassing than dancing. "Calliope," Colonel Clark called my name as he closed in, ensuring that I couldn't just move on and pretend I hadn't seen him. "Bliss, Miranda," he added, polite afterthoughts, as my friends stopped beside me. I should've known he'd be here as a chaperone, but I couldn't imagine why he'd want to talk to me again after it went so un-fantastically the last time.

"What do you think of our handiwork?" He asked, making a proud sweeping gesture to reintroduce us to the decorations we were trying to ignore.

"Handy, for sure. Handy. Handiwork." Bliss's attempt to jump in was more of an awkward stumble off the bench.

"Oh," he said, practically crushed. "I was going for 'wicked cool' here." He was trying so hard, air bunnies and all, that I had to throw him a line before he drowned. "Just so you know, sir, the only people who say 'wicked' are old, or Canadian."

"Ah-ha," he said with an open-handed slap to his own

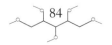

forehead. "Thanks for the tip." I was happy to see him looking almost relaxed and amused. So much so that I thought I might have to thank Miranda for before, when she'd suggested the good deeds.

And speaking of Miranda's better points, the girl was quick to prove she could get us out of a bad situation like nobody's business. "This party is phat, Colonel C; we've gotta get in there ASAP or we'll miss everything," she said, flashing him a sugary smile as she pulled Bliss and I away with her. She really was starting to grow on me – in a fungal kind of way, but not poisonous at least.

For the second time, I followed Miranda and Bliss into the throng, hoping I'd glimpse Jack somewhere in the middle. I was good with crowd-dancing, since I knew I could just keep my steps small and blend in. Miranda threw out one last FYI before she whirled away, "You two owe me for that stellar rescue, by the way!"

Now that we were close enough to see downward of Garrett's head, I had to take a step back and blink repeatedly to avoid being blinded by the red-sequined shirt he'd only buttoned halfway up. Although I did let out a snort, I had to admit he was probably the only guy I'd ever known who could actually carry off that kind of look. When I'd assumed Miranda was going to be the center of the festivities, I'd totally underestimated Garrett's command of the spotlight.

Whereas my dancing style – if you could even call it that – required little space, Garrett ignored all personal boundaries. He was a hundred body parts in perpetual motion, seemingly everywhere at once, so standing back a little was as much for your own safety as enjoyment.

In case we weren't astute enough to decipher all of his spastic gestures, he called out the name of each maneuver as he performed it – "mowing the lawn," "dealing the cards," "making the donuts" (his self-proclaimed "throwback masterpiece"). Each move was more ridiculous than the last, but amazingly all stayed on beat.

When the first strains of a slow song finally cued up, he used "yanking the rope" to mime reeling Bliss in for a dance. *Good for him,* I thought. *And her.* Even in the dark I could tell she was blushing but pleased.

As I backed away from the quickly pairing-off couples, I felt a gentle hand at my elbow. "May I have the pleasure?"

Jack had come dressed to impress in a sharp, dark blue suit, complete with purplish-gray shirt and tie. My face flushed instantly, and I wished for a hard blast of a/c. I also sent a silent thank-you to Bliss for saving me from appearing in jeans or worse.

"Um, the dance, yes," I stuttered, "but the pleasure will

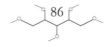

be TBD." My automatic response system had unfortunately not been delayed by my checking him out. I tried to salvage things with a very well-deserved compliment. "You look really great."

"As do you." A total gentleman, he laced his left hand into my right and moved the other to my waist, at the same time guiding my free hand up to his solid shoulder.

He stood only a few inches taller than me, maybe five-foot-nine, which I loved. Tall guys made me feel small and even though I wasn't big on standing out, I didn't want to feel like I was shrinking away, either.

Focus and say something, I urged myself.

"Do you always pack a suit?" I asked, thinking that between him and Bliss, I was going to have to overhaul my entire travel style.

"Don't you know? I'm always ready for anything," he assured me with a grin.

I didn't doubt that for a second.

In the brief pause in conversation, my ears picked out a line from the song playing – something about "falling asleep in those eyes" – and I thought, *Whoever says brown eyes are boring hasn't melted into Jack's soft, chocolaty ones.* Lost in their depth, I was pretty sure I now knew what it felt like to go weak in the knees.

He moved smoothly within our claimed space on the floor, making it easy for me to follow his lead. "So is the belle of the ball enjoying herself?"

My first instinct was, of course, to deflect. "Oh, yeah, Miranda's twirling around out there like a fairy princess."

Another boy might've been taken aback, but Jack was not so easily daunted. "You've always got a comeback slip-knotted at the wharf, ready to launch, don't you?"

Despite my fairy god-conscience yelling, *You actually like this boy, dimwit*, the sarcasm continued to fly out of my mouth, "That's me – Queen of the bark-wit." As soon as the words were out, I vowed yet again to quit smart-assing and start flirting. My thoughts had circled back to him all afternoon, hoping for a moment just like this, and I was ruining it. I could already hear the song coming to an end; our bodies were moving steadily slower and I had to get it together before the music ran out.

But Jack was ready to counter my every foul. "Ah, yes, the lady's bark is sharp, but is her bite?" The final notes drifted away and we stopped swaying, but he didn't take back his hands and neither did I. His eyes were twinkling devilishly as he tilted his head to match his smile. It felt like a dream – sweet, funny, *adorable* Jack looking at *me* like he thought I was those same things. And like he wanted to kiss me.

My whole body braced in anticipation, but then – *boom, boom* – the heavy base opened the next song and Jack was somehow pulled away from me into the crowd as the tempo

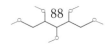

surged up again. I stood stock-still as everyone pulsed around me, kicking myself so hard on the inside that my outside couldn't move. Teddy Geiger had just gifted me four full minutes of one-on-one with Jack Vallard, and I'd completely blown it.

The urge to flee forced my feet into motion and I was out the door faster than even the jocks could've gotten there. The clusters of kids filling the courtyard left my room as the only possibility for escape, so I tried to keep from breaking into a run as I weaved between them and headed for the dorm.

I took the stairs two at a time – not an easy feat in a dress, but I wasn't about to let fashion slow me down. I passed my room and went to the bathroom first to splash water on my face, which was overheated from both the stair-race and the internal browbeating.

The song that'd played over the disastrous scene followed me, haunting me. Its lyrics had infiltrated the moment, particularly the resounding chorus, *For you I will.* As I looked at myself in the mirror and saw a complete disaster – my hair now loose and wild, my cheeks flushed, my lipstick completely chewed off – I couldn't help but feel those words were aimed right at me. As in, *For you, Jack, I will get myself together.* With a sigh, I turned away from the disheartening image.

I started back to my room, surprised to see Janet unlocking her door and looking around as if to make sure she wasn't seen. When she spotted me, our eyes met and she offered a guilty grin. "Okay, you caught me. I snuck over to spy on the party. Don't tell."

"It can be our secret if you'll do me a favor." I remembered that she had a laptop and I wanted to get online quickly before bed.

"I don't negotiate with terrorists," she warned.

"There's just a song I heard tonight," I explained. "I wanted to look up the lyrics."

"I'd love to help you out, but the network is down," she apologized. "Why don't you tell me what you need, and I'll look it up as soon as I can connect out."

I told her the singer's name and part of the chorus – paraphrasing the lines as if I could pretend they weren't emblazoned across my brain.

She tapped a finger to her temple to show she'd noted it in her mental log. "I'll figure it out. So…," she said leadingly, and I cringed. The last thing I wanted to do right now was talk about what'd happened at the dance. "…you liked my music," she finished.

"It was great," I answered with relief. "Everybody was into it."

"Told you so," she teased, wagging a finger at me and some of my dark mood lifted. I let her light words carry me to

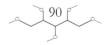

my room to put to bed this awful day.

TEN

*S*unday morning dawned movie-perfect – sun shining, birds chirping – but it still wasn't enough to make me forget about last night's debacle. I knew that everyone in the building was going to want nothing more than to rehash the agonies and ecstasies of the festivities, especially with nothing else on today's schedule, and I had no intention of being around for it. I slipped into a good pay-no-attention-because-there's-nothing-to-see-here ensemble of gray v-neck tee and jean shorts while I mapped out an escape route in my mind.

Peeking out into the hall, I saw that, for once, I was the first one up. I booked it to the stairs and made it down to the ground floor unencountered. Instead of going out the regular way into the high-traffic area, I headed for the emergency door under the stairs that led out the back. The *Warning, Alarm Will Sound* sign no longer served as a deterrent to me, since I'd seen two wrestling guys slam right into the metal bar with no effect.

Finally outside, I felt a rush of giddy pleasure over my stealth exit, only to have it stomped out by a deep voice not two full steps behind me.

"Where're you sneaking off to, Foxy?"

I spun around and was relieved to find Garrett, whom I was sure I'd be able to dismiss pretty easily without any hurt feelings. "I'm not really in the mood to see anyone," I told him in a nice but certain tone.

"Come on, I'm always in the mood to be seen," he argued without missing a beat. *Maybe not such an easy ditch after all.* He threw a long, light arm across my shoulders and steered me away from the building toward a paved path. "Come to my lair, little girl. If you're good, I might even give you some candy."

I rolled my eyes – a seemingly automatic reaction to the opening of his mouth. If anyone were to take him seriously, he'd spend all his time ducking punches.

Deciding that it probably wouldn't be all that torturous of an interrogation, and since he wasn't giving me much choice either, I fell into step beside him. At least I wouldn't have to dig deep for conversation starters – Garrett always had a light and easy subject cued up.

"So you and my boy, Jack, eh?" *So much for small talk.*

There was clearly no point in trying to lie, so I went with

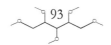

vagueness, hoping to at least draw out what he knew. "Maybe."

"Hoo-hoo, he knocks it out of the park. So, what's he got that I don't?" I relaxed and let the smile overtake my face. I'd forgotten that he was a guy and not inclined to pry for emotional details.

"Um, good grammar?" I suggested mockingly. This was a game I could actually win.

"Real cute, Foxy," he said, using that same nickname again, and I had a sinking feeling that a pattern was being established.

"That's the second time you've called me that," I pointed out.

"Yeah, that's what everyone calls you," he confirmed. "You know, 'cuz you're a snappy little redhead that dives into her hole when the hounds close in."

"Swell," I replied, in no way going to admit that he could be dead right.

"You can thank me for that," he credited himself.

"Oh, sure, because that's exactly what I want to do," I snorted.

"Hey," he defended himself, twisting his draped hand around to tug lightly at my ponytail. "It's the sail here that marked you on the horizon; I just christened the ship."

"So first I'm a fox, then I'm a ship, huh?" I tossed back

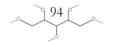

the gimme he'd thrown my way. "I sure get around."

"You do? Right on. The guys'll be amped to hear that." I hadn't even released my full glare when he threw up both hands and laughed, "Kidding!"

"He juggles," I said, going back to the lesser of the two evil topics. "That's what does it for me; it's hot." Only I knew how much truth there was behind my joking.

"Does your girl Bliss go for the clown show, too?" he asked, casually. *Way more interesting territory.*

"I think she goes for dignified behavior – that might be a good starting place for you," I answered, pretty sure she already liked him as-is, but if he wanted to give me a hard time, I felt like I had to return the favor.

He bent over to drag his knuckles on the ground and grunted his solemn pledge, "Gar-rett e-volve." Then he straightened out both his pose and enunciation to add, "I wouldn't complain if you put in a good word for me. Or seven…."

"I've got a bunch of words for you," I offered. "How about, *I'm really not a jackass even though I play one on TV. Help me behave.*"

"So funny, Cyrano de Boobserac," he retorted.

I stopped and looked at him, open-mouthed and indignant, but he went on, unfazed, "Yes, Garrett can read. And

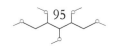

95

also make clever allusions."

"Green light on the reading; octagon at least half the slang and you may get an assist from me." I mimed passing him a ball, which he shot into an imaginary net as we reached the front steps of the gym.

"Wow," I said, too awed by the impressive glass structure to even worry much about my rumpled reflection in the mirrored façade. Unlike the two places my campus life had revolved around so far, this building was clearly brand new. And nothing at all like the window-less brick box that I pictured when I heard the word, "gym." *Arena* came to mind now, along with *modern art*.

"This is nothing; you gotta see the inside. It's badass, man." He flashed me the Gene Simmons tongue, then assumed a professorial pose. "And architecturally superior as well."

I let myself be lured in only when the silence confirmed that there was no one else inside, and was immediately stunned by how right he was. For the second time this week, my jaw actually dropped open in amazement.

Inside, all four stories were wide open, the space extending easily as long as a football field. The ice-blue floor stretched to all four corners, reflecting the bright blue above, and the way the slightly-tinted glass connected the floor to the ceiling on every side made me feel like I was suspended in a box of sky.

The only furnishings to ground the floating sensation

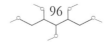

were a dozen rows of padded bleachers across the far end. They were presumably more for resting athletes than spectators, though the idea that there may be an exhibition in here for the rest of us at some point was definitely exciting. Besides Garrett's own self-promotion, I'd heard the rumors about how impressively the athletes were performing here on campus, and I wanted to see for myself.

"Watch this." A few feet to the right of the door, Garrett hit the center of a wall-mounted dial and the clear floor went dark, cancelling the ice-like effect. Then LED lights appeared, shining up through the floor to mark yard lines and end zones as clearly as if they'd been painted on. The Army insignia with its flags and cannons served as the home team logo at center field.

I'd barely absorbed the transformation when he turned the knob one click, simultaneously erasing all the football designations and activating a new set of lights across the middle third of the building – these creating the foul-lanes and three-point curves of a full basketball court.

Another twist revealed a perfect baseball diamond, and Garrett's eyes lit up to show off his favorite toy. "Wondering how we could swing full throttle and not shatter the glass?" he asked, not waiting for a response. "Check this out." He pushed a bright green button and one entire long wall began to glide silently upward like an electric garage door until it came to rest flush across the ceiling.

"Unbe-freaking-lievable," I breathed, while taking it all in. Then I suddenly thought to ask, "Are you supposed to be touching all this stuff?"

"Of course," he laughed. "It's open twenty-four-seven so we can practice or fool around as much as we want. Isn't it wild?" He rocked back on his heels, and if his thumbs hadn't been hooked into the waistband of his shorts, I was pretty sure he'd have clapped with glee. "They said this was an athlete's paradise, but I had no idea. Bet you're jealous of my little kingdom."

"Yeah, our group doesn't really need a facility or anything," I said. But even as phenomenal as this space was, our fresh-air sessions better suited me.

"Well, we can't get enough of this place. It's like a dream." The image he launched meshed perfectly with the airy atmosphere.

"How do you drag yourselves out for meals?" I asked, only half-teasing.

"It does take some serious fuel to maintain this formidable physique," he agreed, reminding me not to underestimate the gastric needs of the teenage boy.

Right then, two guys came jogging down the path, ready to work out, and I told Garrett that was my signal to get going.

"Until we meet again, mi-lady," he excused me with a

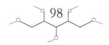

gallant bow.

"Fo-shizzle," I sassed, playing against type as he had.

I walked away, not knowing why but feeling almost buoyant, as if all were now right with the world. I smiled at the realization that, despite all the non-answers and weirdness, this was how it felt to really fit somewhere.

Reveling in my happy thoughts, I decided to take advantage of the unscheduled day and veg. I drifted off the main path toward the edge of the woods, looking for a good spot to stretch out and just watch the puffy clouds parade by. The grass was cool and soft on my back as I lay down on it – not luxurious enough to camp on without a pad or anything, but plenty comfy for a dreambreak.

I'd barely laced my hands behind my head and closed my eyes when I heard voices seemingly only feet away. My first thought was to stand up and alert the fellow nature lovers to my existence before I got accidentally trampled, but for some reason my gut instinct kept me pinned to the ground long enough for me to realize that silence was the right choice.

"You're sure none of them know?" The first voice was husky and male, but too low to reveal anything else about the speaker.

"Not a clue." The second voice spoke even lower still, so much so that I couldn't even tell if it was a guy or a girl.

"The jocks are all so over-inflated, they just think it's proof they should all go pro." The conspirators shared a snicker between them.

"Arty kids, too. They just assume the others steer clear because they always have. That might be as much anti-socialness as talent, though." I'd heard the art/music group being referred to as "heavies" because they were all so dark and introspective that they almost walled out everybody else, but it seemed like this conversation was about more than just that.

And as for the jocks, I thought, *if something wild was happening with them, Garrett definitely would've mentioned it.*

"How can the vanishing ones not figure it out? There's a million of them." *Yeah, person number one*, I asked in my mind, *what're we all missing?*

"You've seen the tapes – they're like a herd of sheep." *Hey, person number two*, I inwardly scolded, *that was cold.*

"Either none of them pay enough attention to see it," the second voice continued, "or since everyone's doing it, only an outsider would notice."

"Let's hope it stays that way." The first person's concern was apparent even in his whisper.

"It will as long as we keep our heads down and our mouths shut," speaker number two ordered, not that it helped me to identify them. I strained my ears for more and heard,

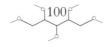

"Someone's coming. Do not contact me; I'll get to you when I can."

Please do not come this way, I prayed silently, keeping my eyes closed. Then I abruptly changed my mind. *No, wait!* I thought. *Open your eyes to see who it is!* I looked up in time to catch the tail of a shadow pass into the treeline and that was all. I could tell by the path of retreat that at least he hadn't come close enough to see me either, which was some relief.

I sat there, stunned, not sure what else to do but replay the conversation in my mind. I tried to make sense of what I'd overheard; it seemed clear that something was happening – that we were all *doing* something – without our knowing. And whoever had seen it wanted us to stay in the dark. *Could this have anything to do with the cameras? Videos?* I knew I sure hadn't been invited to any viewing parties.

I definitely needed more information, *but where to get it?* Colonel Clark said I could always go to him, but if things were intentionally being kept from the kids, surely the boss had to be in on it. *Who knew what he knew?* No, going to him was not an option.

I thought of Bliss, Miranda, Garrett, and Jack – of course I should tell them. *But tell them what?* I didn't have any facts or names – what if they just thought I'd misheard the whole thing? *Or imagined it?* I didn't want them to think I was crazy – I just *got* them.

I flipped back and forth in my mind like I was picking petals off a daisy – *they'll still like me…no, they'll think I'm nuts; they'll still be my friends…or they'll dump me like last year's cell phone.*

I couldn't see a clear answer. Between this new complication, whatever was going on with Jack, and getting ready for tomorrow's group session…*oh, and the teeny tiny other worry that kept getting pushed to the back of my thoughts behind all the other drama – the possibility that I might actually be filled with Jell-o instead of human stuff inside*…I was too fried to do anything about anything right now.

Tomorrow, I promised myself, *I'll definitely figure out at least one thing tomorrow. I hope.*

ELEVEN

*H*eading out for group session Monday morning, I opened my door and almost crashed into the barricade formed by a concerned Bliss and an angry Miranda.

"Where have you been?" Miranda attacked first.

Bliss's opener was a little gentler and a lot more exciting to hear. "Jack asked about you yesterday," she chirped. "At breakfast."

"You fully bailed on the dance and have been MIA ever since," Miranda lectured, clearly having not been finished.

"And again at dinner," Bliss added, continuing to play good cop.

"Yeah, and freaking tea time and midnight snack; we get it," interjected the bad cop. The volleying would've been comical if I wasn't so busy thinking about what I was going to say when my turn came up.

"He gave me a note for you, but it's in my room," Bliss went on. "I didn't read it; I just didn't want to carry it around since I didn't know when I'd run into you again." That was a guilt trip bigger than I'd packed for.

"What did you do to the poor boy?" Miranda asked, her curiosity now captured by the mention of a private note. She was clearly more intrigued by its contents than concerned for Jack's well-being.

"Earnhardt and Gordon, can you come in for a pit stop, please?" I took advantage of the brief ceasefire to get in a few words and start moving us all downstairs.

I should've known Miranda wouldn't even pause long enough to appreciate my joke. "Don't play with us, Miss Ditch. I would've told Quirk you'd gone AWOL if I hadn't heard you rustling around in your room last night. And yes, I knocked, and yes, I know you pretended not to be in there."

"That was you?" I tried to play dumb. "Sorry, I was trying to call my mom and the phone cord doesn't reach the door."

"I've been calling home all weekend, but I get the machine every time," Bliss piped up. "It's kinda weird, too, because I thought my dad would've called me back by now," Miranda may not have bought my excuse, but Bliss was more than happy to move past the conflict and just be friends again.

"Yeah, my mom's been out, too," I said, relieved to not

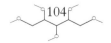

be the only one. "I mean, I knew she'd be running to signing events and meetings, but she should've checked in."

Miranda remained unconcerned. "Hello!" she shouted. "The parentals are so psyched to be free that they're partying like it's spring break in Cabo."

Bliss laughed, lightly at first, but then it started getting away from her. A minute later, tears were streaming down her face. "I just pictured my mother," she gasped, "in a whipped-cream bikini." She doubled over, trying to catch her breath. "I think I'm gonna pee my pants."

By now we were almost on top of the meeting area, and I patted myself on the back for getting through the walk fairly unscathed. However, I also hadn't had a chance to tell them to keep their eyes open for anything strange at today's session. Then again, maybe it'd be better that I was the only one on alert today. This way, if I saw anything interesting it'd help substantiate what I'd overheard yesterday when I finally shared the story with my friends. And best case scenario, something totally remarkable would happen and give me more info, plus distract Miranda and Bliss from resuming their interrogation about Jack later.

I needn't have worried; if wishes were horses, I was galloping out of the gate before the starting gun.

Everyone took their usual places so quickly that the three of us got stuck in the front again, and I didn't want to cause a

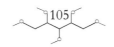

scene by trying to move. Maybe I wouldn't be able to see anyone behind me, but I could try to utilize my other senses – listen for chatter, rustling – and maybe get a feel for where Janet was so that I could steal a glance around.

But, soon enough, that plan was also dead in the water. Not two minutes into "focus time," I was startled by applause from the back. All sixty-eight of us turned as one to see who'd caused the interruption.

"Can we help you?" boomed Janet from the front, the thunder of her voice rolling over our heads to reach Jack, whose hands immediately froze mid-clap and retreated to his jeans pockets.

"Sorry," he said with a sheepish grin. "I just wanted to say, well, *wow*."

Murmurs immediately rippled down the rows about what wow-worthy event we'd all missed.

And back-to-business Janet was having none of it. "Why are you disrupting our session, Mr. Vallard?"

"It's just Jack," he answered, a friendly dog wagging its tail in front of a hungry tiger.

"I am well aware of who you are," she snapped. "Now tell me why you are *here*." I couldn't help but squirm for him. Although she was usually so easygoing with us, the officer in Janet did not appreciate his disruption of her routine.

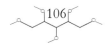

I shouldn't have worried for him, though – Jack knew the score and didn't take her hostility personally. "I apologize, Captain Quirk. They haven't decided exactly where to place me, so Colonel Clark told me to try out all the groups and see what fits. So here I am."

Janet swallowed hard in acceptance of orders issued by her superior officer. "Very well," she agreed, though not agreeably. For now, you will remain off to the side and observe." Still a little peeved at the interruption, she apparently wasn't going to waste time bringing him up to speed.

Jack, on the other hand, wasn't quite ready to be silenced. "Could everyone do this right away? Or did it take practice?" His questions came out of fascination rather than rudeness, but Janet was clearly out of patience.

"Mr. Vallard, if you could please observe silently so we may continue…," she tried futilely to regain control over the now chattering group.

As if commanded to do so, everyone returned to what they were just doing – trying to disappear. Only this time, they were also checking out their neighbors to try and figure out what was going on – what had so impressed the cute brown-haired boy with the great smile. Within moments, mumblings and gasps audibled the various reactions.

The result was a buzz of confusion, as most didn't know

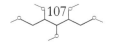

what they were supposed to be looking for. The gasps were clustered around a select few kids – one of the gasps being mine, and one of the select few being Bliss.

I only knew it was actually Bliss beside me because she'd been standing there just seconds before and hadn't had time to go anywhere else. I stood shock-still at the sight of her encased in an almost-ethereal glow. And then she disappeared completely into the light, as if a shooting star had fallen from the top of her head all the way down to her Skechers, engulfing her.

But as soon as she saw not just me staring at her, but the gathering, gawking crowd, she flipped off the shine like a light switch.

Janet pushed her way to Bliss's side and, even though I'd have bet money that she was going to clap her hands and call us to order, she just stood there as wide-eyed as the rest of us.

"How did you do that?" she finally breathed in amazement, at the same time reaching out dazedly to touch Bliss's forearm and confirm that she was, in fact, real. Then she scanned the crowd, picking out the individuals at the centers of the other five circles. "Kimberly, Andrea, Erin, Susan, Juliana," she called, having regained her composure, "come to the front." Her hand closing around Bliss's arm, she added, "You, too."

When all six girls had made their way to her, she gave the one-word command: "Again."

The girls obediently complied, producing a stunning result. Those of us closest to the spectacle were almost blinded by the six-fold magnitude of light; it was like we were standing too close to the sun, but also unable to look away. It was worse than not being able to see; I felt like I couldn't even think. Or breathe.

Bliss, in her infinite shyness, was the first to turn her glow off again. The rest of the girls soon followed suit, although I could tell that some were more reluctant than others to relinquish the intense admiration of the crowd.

"This certainly gives us a great deal to consider," Janet said, snapping everyone back to reality. "You," she paused, contemplating the central six and then assigning them a designation, "*stars*. Stay here. Everyone else is dismissed. And out of respect for your peers, you will not discuss today's session outside the group. We'll reconvene here tomorrow at nine a.m."

Any other group of teenagers would've booked it back to the dorm – and out of Janet's earshot – to spill every detail, but the combination of total awe along with a lifetime spent following orders rendered everyone virtually silent.

Check that – everyone but Miranda, who was fuming. Loudly. "You've got to be kidding me," she growled and I cringed with fear that flames were about to shoot out of her nostrils. "Those girls? Stars? And not me? Guess again! Miranda

Taylor is sure as heck more stellar than any one of those twits." I said nothing, knowing at this point that trying to talk to her would be like trying to feed chicken to a bear – no matter how much sense it made to me, the bear was more likely to bite off my head instead.

"And Bliss can consider her little blip off my radar for sure," she raged on. "She is so dead to me."

That I couldn't let pass. "Miranda, you know that being singled out is the last thing Bliss wants. You can't blame her." But my words were thrashed in the wake of her full-throttle departure.

Vowing to try to talk to her again once things had simmered down, I turned my attention to Bliss to see if I could give her any support. Unfortunately, Janet had already closed ranks, making it clear that the dismissal order left no room for exceptions.

All I knew was that Garrett had to be having a better time in his Monday group session than the rest of us were in this one. *Honestly, even if the ceiling of the arena fell in and shattered across the floor, it'd still be better than this disaster.* With two unhappy friends, and the inability to help either one, I decided to go back to my own room and think over the day's drama.

"Hey, I've been looking for you." In all the commotion, I'd totally forgotten Jack was there. Now with him standing just inches away, I couldn't figure out how that was even possible.

"Really?" I tried to act like I hadn't known and that hearing it this morning hadn't made my whole day. Not to mention what hearing it straight from his lips was doing to me now.

"Yeah," he said with his usual easy smile. "Did Bliss give you my note?"

"No," I answered, looking back once more to where Janet still held the newly discovered "stars" in a tight group. "And I don't think I'll be getting to her anytime soon."

"No big deal," he said, lightly touching my arm. "There's just something I want to show you. Can you come to my room after dinner?"

Ab-so-lutely, I thought, inwardly jumping up and down, *and if you keep smiling at me like that, I will eat glass while walking over hot coals to get there.*

"Mm-hmm," I finally answered, deciding it'd be better to just nod and not actually open my mouth and risk my thoughts spilling out. *Why did he have such an overwhelming effect on me? And how?* His eyes burned away my thoughts in a way that was ten times worse than being blinded by the stars.

"Great." His hand slid down my arm and gave my hand a quick squeeze before letting go. "I've got some things to finish up, so I'll see you later," he said with a *wink*, which from any other male under sixty-five would've been borderline creepy, but on Jack, of course, was adorable and summoned all the butterflies in my stomach to flight.

How about that? I thought, then stopped before I over-thunk the excitement right out of it.

The day may have been horrifically derailed by the train wreck between Miranda and Bliss, but now the evening sure looked like it was right on track.

TWELVE

*A*t eight o'clock, I stood in front of Jack's door, nervous not only about seeing him alone, but also because I wasn't sure if I was even allowed to be on the boys' floor. I'd planned to ask someone at dinner if there were rules about this stuff, but I'd ended up eating alone since Bliss and Miranda were avoiding each other, Jack was finishing up his secret something and Garrett was still on the court with his second-string BFF, Nate. And on top of that, all the alone-ness had given me so much time to over-think and worry that I hadn't even been able to eat.

Almost the same instant I touched it, the door flew open. "Welcome to my parlor," Jack greeted me, pulling the handle toward him. "Said the spider to the fly," he finished, stepping backward into his room and making a sweeping invitation with his free hand.

"And 'tis the prettiest little parlor that I ever did spy," I quoted back, thankful that my mouth had been able to spit out the next line of the poem while my brain struggled to catch up. *How did he seem to know everything?* I wondered. It caught me off-guard to hear the quirky rhyme, so I asked, "Is your mom a writer, too? Is that how you know Mary Howitt?"

"No, I picked that one up all on my own," he said, dipping his shoulders in the slightest charming bow. "I like to think of myself as a kind of Renaissance guy."

"From court jester to romantic bard – you've got quite a range," I commented, happy to feel my nerves starting to settle down enough to give me a fighting chance at being charming, too.

"Well, if you know a little about a lot of different things, you have something to talk about with everyone you meet," he explained.

"I wish I could talk to people," I said softly, my private thought making its own way out loud.

"You do alright with me," he answered simply, and there it was, again – that easy smile that could wrap me up and knock me over, all at once.

"Crazy, right? So…where's all your stuff?" I asked, moving on to check out the neat but pretty spartan room.

He shrugged as he answered, "I'm not really into stuff. I

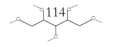

feel like it kind of gets in my way."

"Not junk, but books at least," I clarified. "I mean, everybody reads." I left off, *Everybody interesting, anyway,* in case for some bizarre reason he had something against books.

He eased around me to pull open the top drawer of his dresser. "Who needs bookshelves when you've got extra drawers?" I peered over his shoulder and sure enough, instead of socks or shirts were a couple dozen paperbacks lined up like a vertical file. "I'm no fashionmista, and I like to find new uses for stuff, so there you go."

He may be right about his style not being flashy or brand-y, but that sure didn't take away from how good he looked in his classic solid navy tee and *very* well-fitting dark jeans. I couldn't help thinking he'd be a great J. Crew model, but before my thoughts drifted too far into images of him gazing broodingly from a cliff along the rocky coastline, I yanked myself back to the present.

I picked up the frame from the top of his dresser and examined his family in the black and white photo. In the middle, his mom was sitting on his dad's lap, her arms around his neck, and Jack and his two sisters sprawled around them on the couch, all five with the same dark hair and Cheshire smiles. It didn't seem to be any particular occasion or holiday, just a scene made special by their obvious closeness as a unit.

"You look just like your mom," I noted.

"Really?" He cocked one eyebrow in faux offense.

"The guy version, obviously." I rolled my eyes and put the frame back down, then leaned in to read the screen on the iPod docked next to it. "What's playing?" The tune was jazzy but young and fresh with a kind of crossover-pop feel to it.

"Cool, right?" I could tell he was really into the music by the way his face lit up as he started telling me about it. "It's Jamie Cullum – *Heard It All Before*. This is his first album from back in the nineties and he only put out like five hundred copies. I bid on three other discs online before I finally scored this one."

"Shows commitment," I acknowledged the admirable trait.

"To everything that makes me happy," he agreed. "Don't worry; you can come up here and listen any time you need a good music fix. Mi studio es su studio," he issued an invitation that I would absolutely take him up on in the future.

"If you're so into music, how come you don't go with that group?" I asked, hoping it was okay to.

"Those guys are pros," he answered, and I waited to see where he was going with it. "I like music, and I fool around with it, but the heavies take it a little too seriously to have an amateur like me hanging around."

"Serious" was a much more diplomatic way of putting it

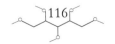

that I ever could've come up with. It made me wonder if he was just that nice of a guy, or if he knew some of the kids in the group.

"Are there any around here?" I asked, adding quickly, "Heavies, I mean. On your floor." *Please don't let him think that sounded as stupid as I think it did*, I pleaded silently.

"No," he answered, looking at me curiously. "They're all girls; didn't you know that?"

"Uh-uh," I admitted. "I really don't know anybody besides you, Garrett, Bliss, and Miranda." I had a feeling that didn't make any sense to Jack, who'd probably gone out of his way to meet everyone on campus. And knowing that included like eighty other girls who probably did not say dumb things every time they opened their mouths didn't make me feel any better about it. Looked like *meet new people* should be the next item on my to-do list. *Right after getting Jack to like me*, I amended.

Searching for a change of subject, I asked, "So why's your comforter in the middle of the floor?"

He rubbed his hands together like a magician. Or a villain. Maybe both. "Ah, she finally gets to the interesting question," he said before lowering himself onto the nondescript black spread and reaching one hand up to pull me lightly down beside him. "You're going to have to lay down for the presentation, and I thought you might be a little weirded out to come in here and sprawl across my bed with me."

You have no idea, I thought to myself, swallowing hard. Trying to sound breezy I asked, "There's a show?"

Jack cocked his head slightly toward me and asked, "Why did you think I asked you to come up here?"

"I really had no idea," I answered, sticking with the surface truth and not giving away all my lurid hopes for the reason behind the invite.

"And you came anyway," he laughed wickedly, but gently took my elbow to ease me onto my back. At the same time, he slid his pillow beneath my head, then lay down right beside me, his arm lined up shoulder-to-elbow with mine, our hips and knees likewise connected.

Don't hyperventilate, don't hyperventilate, I repeated like a mantra at least a dozen times in a second, certain that I was not going to get a third shot at this and could not blow it again.

Thankfully, Jack didn't seem aware of my inner distress as he clicked a button on a cord that appeared from somewhere in his far hand and the lights went out.

I needed a second to process what I was seeing; the immediate darkness from the lights turning off was quickly punctuated with a dozen or so twinkling points of light directly above me. As my eyes adjusted, I realized I was looking at a carefully arranged string of Christmas-light stars somehow shining through the ceiling.

I could feel him waiting for my reaction, but I had no words. I'd always wanted to go to a planetarium, and I had a feeling this was what it'd be like, only here there was privacy, intimacy, *Jack*. "It's breathtaking," I finally managed to whisper, followed by, "Word-taking, too, I guess." I cringed at my own inadequacy for romantic situations. And no doubt about it, this was epic romance brought to life.

"Do you know what you're looking at?" Jack prompted after several minutes, hesitant to break the peaceful silence.

"Um...stars?" I ventured, wondering if it was a trick question.

Gentleman Jack of course passed on the opportunity to call me out as a master of the obvious and asked next, "Do you remember when we met and you told me you didn't really like your name, but I said that I thought it was pretty great?" I nodded encouragingly so that he would continue. "Well, I got this great visual right then of bringing the constellation of Calliope to life. So you could see the beauty of it."

"That's what this is?" *How amazingly sweet.*

"Well, no," he laughed. "I came back and Googled it and found that, unfortunately, there is no actual constellation for Calliope."

"For real? I always thought there were constellations for

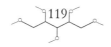

all the myth-people, like there're planets for all the gods, right?" *You totally should've known better!* I berated myself.

"Yeah, not so much," he replied. "Not even Kalliope with a *K*, or Clio, or anything about the muses, even. There's an asteroid – Kalliope 22 – but it looks like a lumpy gray rock-blob, so I didn't think that was the way to go."

"Sounds like a good call," I agreed. "So what am I looking at then?" He'd aroused my curiosity now more than ever.

"It's Virgo," he explained. "I read that the muses were beautiful virgins and that Virgo's supposed to represent all women. It's a stretch, I know." His tone teetered toward self-doubt, but he pushed past it. "You start here," he began, pointing up toward the right-most star, then drew in the air down and around – tracing an outline back to the beginning. "It's a woman in a long dress with outstretched arms."

"Wow, I can see her," I whispered, not wanting to break the spell.

"That brightest star, there," he said, pointing again, "Spica, makes it pretty easy to find in the sky, too."

"It's fantastic," I said. "Truly. How did you find the time?"

"I still don't have any special *ability* to work on," he said, revealing a brief flash of unsurety for only the second time since I'd met him. And I took it as a good sign that both instances had

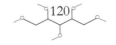

been tonight, when we were alone. Maybe I wasn't the only nervous one in the room. "So I have a lot of unassigned time here," he went on. "Like pretty much all day, if I want."

"The talent…and vision…," I trailed off, shaking my head, still stunned by the enormity of it all. "I can't believe you did all this. For me." *This is what it feels like to be honored*, I thought, my throat thick.

"I think you're worth it," he said simply, taking my hand and lacing his strong fingers between mine. With my eyes still trained on the ceiling, I felt, rather than saw his head turn toward me. My racing heart screeched to a halt and for an instant I wasn't sure I was still on the planet.

I slowly turned my face to meet his and found him impossibly close. It was so intensely still that when he blinked his eyes, his long lashes fluttered a breeze across my face. I felt the current buzzing between our side-by-side limbs and I was sure that even the slightest movement would ignite the inevitable spark, would roar into an engulfing flame.

If he'd been cautious about making the wrong rushed move so far tonight, that hesitation was long gone as his warm lips smoothly met mine. His kiss was everything I'd hoped it would be – confident and strong, but without the intent to conquer. He didn't so much claim my mouth as draw it to his, calling me to join him at a mutual center.

And instead of the dizzying, disabling weakness I'd expected to feel, fierce desire surged up through my being to answer him – the tide responding to the moon. Without breaking the bond, I turned the rest of my body toward him, curling into the curve of his side. My hands moved of their own accord – one sliding up the smooth cotton of his shirt to land lightly on the right side of his chest; the other, still entwined with his, pulled both up to rest between my breasts and his left side, a bridge between our hearts.

His free hand combed through my hair from the side of my face to the back of my head, and his fingertips brushed the back of my neck, sending stars down my spine, and all my worries over the dance washed away beneath the wave of him.

This was how it was supposed to happen; this was our first kiss as it was *meant to be*, not some awkward peck in the middle of a loud, crowded dance floor. That would've been forced, and fast, and fully unmemorable, which I was suddenly sure Jack had known all along. He'd wanted and waited to make it perfect. And it was.

THIRTEEN

"Yo, J, did she go flabgast or what?" All of a sudden, the door banged open and Garrett busted in like a monsoon on Mardi Gras. And he un-graciously brought with him the bright light of the hallway to fully showcase my less-than-presentable state. Besides my wrinkly shirt and tangled hair, I was still sprawled half on top of Jack in the middle of the floor.

I sat up and made a half-hearted attempt to pull myself together, but who was I trying to fool, really? And to be honest, I was so ticked at Garrett for barging in that I didn't have the extra energy to summon up real embarrassment.

I kept my mouth clenched shut, but my mind hollered at him, *Can't you see we're a little busy here? We may be fully clothed, but please have the decency to back out and close the door behind you.*

"Oh, hey, Foxy – you're still here, so I can ask you myself

– you down with the up?" Garrett tilted his head back to take in the starry sky. He couldn't seriously think I wanted to have a conversation right now, could he? It seemed all yesterday's togetherness had done nothing to facilitate our telepathic communication.

Totally fine with a one-sided exchange, he went right on talking. "I saw J-Bird pulling down the tiles and offered my assistance; the six-half and the bounce came in mighty handy." Garrett jumped up lightly and popped loose an unlighted ceiling square to demonstrate. "And my comrade Nate snagged us a screwdriver to slam the holes." I had a vague recollection of the teammate Garrett was talking about, but less than zero interest in sharpening that image at the moment.

"That rocked, 'cause it's not like we could go to our exalted mentor for an assist," Garrett went on. "Although, Lurkin' Larson does have a roxor watch that gives the temp and odds of a rain-out; I gotta get me one of those. He's still a tool, though. And not the constructive kind."

Spell officially broken, I groaned inwardly. *Time to call it a night.*

"Have you met Nate? The hoopster with the sick one-eighty slam?" Garrett asked me, as if that description would paint a wanted-poster-clear picture of the guy. I didn't answer and Jack blew out a sigh as he rustled himself up to standing, equally

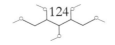

124

resigned to the end of our date.

When Garrett said, "Lemme go get him," Jack was quick to pull me up beside him and offer, "I'll walk you back to your room."

I checked my watch and was shocked to find it was almost midnight. *Wow, good fun sure can make the minutes – or hours – fly,* I thought. "No, it's really late," I said, then reminded him, "I'm right across the hall from Janet. After today, I think you need to keep a low profile around her."

"Right, okay," he agreed, though I was happy to see it was reluctantly. "I'll see you tomorrow?"

"Absolutely." I hoped that he was better at reading my thoughts than Garrett and that my grim smile portrayed my disappointment with the untimely departure. And our goodbye might as well be a handshake with our self-appointed chaperone still standing guard.

"G'night," he said softly, holding the door to the stairwell for me. I felt his eyes follow as I made my way as stealthily as I could up the two flights to my floor.

At the top, I was met with total silence and an empty hallway, but I couldn't make myself go into my room. Way too keyed-up to even think about sleeping, I tiptoed down to see Bliss instead.

I knocked lightly but deliberately as I whispered into the

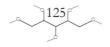

crack, "Bliss? Are you still awake?" I heard some rustling, muffled footsteps, and then she appeared at the door with the bleary eyes of a rude awakening. Luckily, when she saw my goofy grin she brightened instantly, grabbed my hand, and pulled me inside. "Well, aren't you just a hot mess?" she said. "You better get in here and make it worth my while for waking me up."

She snapped on her bedside lamp and I looked around, realizing that I'd never actually been in here before since she always came by my room on her way in or out. The room was fun and trendy and well put-together, but it just seemed…not *her*. Everything was very pinky-orange, from the pillows, to the sheets, to the sheer curtains – even the stripes on the zebra-patterned rug. I couldn't put my finger on it, but something just felt off.

"Funky, huh?" Bliss said with a wry smile. Apparently I hadn't masked my uncertainty over the décor as well as I thought.

I shrugged my shoulders, not quite knowing what to say. "It just doesn't feel like you."

She laughed ironically. "Because it's not."

"They didn't do your room here like you have it at home?" I asked, not understanding.

"Oh no, this is exactly the same as in San Antonio, but I sure didn't choose any of it." She answered, wrinkling her nose in distaste.

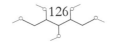

When she realized that I was waiting for the rest of the story, she continued, "Last year when election-time was gearing up, everyone was hot for good deployment and military stories, so some people, like my mom, became kind of pseudo-celebrities. You know, since she's important and beautiful and all, everyone wanted an interview. One magazine photographer said we needed better 'staging,' and, next thing you know, I had designer digs." She waved at the results, then pointed to the poster of the Jonas Brothers mounted by the door. "I don't even really know who they are. I listen to country music, but *Ricola* – yes, like the cough drop – said they were 'now' so that's what I got."

I'd had a decent amount of experience myself with interviewers and photographers because of my mom, but this was a whole new level and I told her so.

"Don't I know it? No joke – she told me the theme was *Sweet Sixteen in Tangerine*." She barely got out the line with a straight face.

"Of course," I said, rolling my eyes appreciatively. "Everyone knows orange is the new pink."

Next she gestured toward the photo-decoupaged desk. "Those aren't even my pictures; the photographer brought in a box of random shoot leftovers. Totally more *scary* than *sweet*, right?" she asked rhetorically as she flopped onto the bed with a snort.

"Well, that's because you're sophisticated *seventeen* now," I said, climbing up beside her and pulling one of the shaggy pillows onto my lap. "You should call them back for an upgrade." We both cracked up again, this time the laughter building until we could barely breathe.

When we finally settled down, bloodhound Bliss was back on the scent. "So don't even try to tell me you came to my room in the middle of the night to judge my style."

"Well…," I stalled to draw out the suspense.

"Dish." Bliss was having none of it. "Now."

"Okay," I agreed; I wasn't going to make her beg. "I just came from Jack's room." If I wasn't still on such a high, I would've been embarrassed at my sing-songy voice.

"Uh, rewind!" She demanded, leaning closer. "How did said scenario transpire?"

"That note he gave you was an invite," I hedged, smirking.

"Oooh, I knew I should've read it!" she squealed. "Sooo? Details, please."

"He made me a constellation," I said, knowing I was being almost torturously vague, but unable to help myself. It's not like this kind of thing happened to me all the time. Or that I'd ever had a good girlfriend to share it with.

"What?" She grabbed me by the shoulders, shaking me

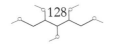

with her own excitement.

"With lights embedded in his ceiling," I started to explain, then went on to describe the creation in more detail so she could visualize.

"That is sooo romantic," she drawled, throwing herself back onto her pillow in a swooning faint when I was done. "He's such a doll."

"I know, right?" I was so giddy that I clapped my hands together like a little girl.

Bliss suddenly bolted back upright as if something had just occurred to her. "So was there more than stargazing?"

"Some...," I admitted, but offered nothing further. Certain details of the evening I just wanted to keep for myself. Plus, in reality, we'd done just as much talking as making out, anyway. And I was proud to note that my half of the exchange was almost all clever and non-moronic.

As I wrapped up my story, telling Bliss how I'd walked back by myself to keep Jack away from Janet, I started feeling guilty for going on and on without even asking about her big drama.

"You had a pretty crazy day, too, huh?" I opened gently, in case she didn't feel up to talking about it yet.

"Yeah, and Janet kept us forever," she vented. "I thought it was time to call in the National Guard for a rescue, except that,

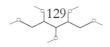

well, she *is* the National Guard."

"So did you feel funny when you did – whatever it is that you did?" *What're we calling it anyway?* I wondered. *'Starring' it up?*

"I didn't feel anything," she griped. "You know how we agreed that nothing was happening in last week's sessions? Today was still like that for me. That girl Andrea said she was sizzling like a firecracker, but I think she's full of it."

"Did you know anything was happening at all?" I didn't want to pry but the whole thing was so amazing – *how could I not?*

"All I knew was that everyone – including you – was staring at me like I had two heads," she reprimanded.

"Sorry, but have you seen yourself?" I asked. "I mean, did you come back here and try it in the mirror or anything?"

"Yeah," she admitted, "but I'm not sure I can see what y'all saw. After a while, I thought I kind of looked like I rolled around in sparkly eye shadow, but I think I was just imagining it." She shrugged, not very impressed with herself.

"Wow," I said, then repeated it, "*Wow.* No, it's way, *way* better than that. Try comet, supernova – I don't know, I can't even explain it to you." I found myself with no words to do her transformation justice.

"Then maybe I'm better off not seeing it." She took a long pause and I debated whether I should ask more questions or drop the topic, but she decided for me.

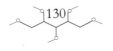

"Just don't ask for a demonstration right now. Performing on command is starting to make me feel like a show dog."

I nodded, point taken.

"How's Miranda?" she asked hesitantly after a quiet minute. "Is she still mad at me?"

"I don't know; she took off after group. Why would you think she's mad at you?" I'd wondered if we were going to go there and so just wanted to diffuse the situation.

"How could I not?" she pointed out. "I was only like five yards away when she screamed at you that I was dead to her."

I hadn't realized Bliss had heard the tirade. "You know Miranda," I said. "She's jealous and she's pissed, but she'll get over it. I mean, if you frown for too long those creases will freeze in your forehead forever, right?" We shared a hopeful smile and I took that to mean she was okay enough to wait and see.

"How does Jack know so much about astronomy, anyway?" she flipped the subject back.

"He looked it up online," I told her.

"He couldn't have," she disagreed, shaking her head. "Servers are down."

"They must've come back up today," I answered, assuming that was what'd happened.

"No, I tried to check my e-mail on my laptop right before

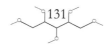

bed," she countered again. "Nothing."

"Weird. Must be off and on?" I paused for a minute, then said, "Speaking of weird, I kind of overheard something yesterday that was a little fishy...."

"Aren't you just the Queen of big reveals tonight? We should've called Maury." She reached over and patted my hand. "I'm teasing! I'm just glad you finally came out of hiding." She knew I'd fill her in about my dance disaster eventually, but we both knew this was not the time. She brought us back to the matter at hand, asking, "So what'd you hear?"

I relayed the conversation to the best of my memory, continually flipping back and forth in my mind as I spoke as to whether I had an overactive imagination or if there really was something shady to be worried about.

Bliss, however, was instantly ready to put all her money on the latter. "This is bad, Clio! We've got to find out who it was and what they're up to!" Her voice rose to the edge of panic.

"But what if I heard wrong? What if it's nothing?" I said more than asked, trying to keep her calm.

"You and I both know it's not nothing. Now we have to find out what it is," she asserted, making me very glad I'd confided in her.

"How?" I asked. "I wouldn't even know where to begin."

Bliss wasn't worried about that. "We don't have to do all

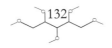

the digging ourselves, you kook. We have help."

"I don't want them to think I'm nuts." We were both of course talking about Miranda, Garrett, and, most importantly, Jack.

"Clio, if you can't see that you have some real friends here, then you really are nuts," Bliss said matter-of-factly.

"Okay, General Campbell," I put myself in her service. "What's our first move?"

"We're going to do what any good soldiers would do, Private Kaid," she ordered. "Let's rally the troops."

FOURTEEN

*T*he launch of our operation was unavoidably delayed when I opened my door in the morning and almost tripped over a breakfast basket with an order to report directly to the health center stapled on top. A glance down the hallway confirmed that everyone had gotten one, so my first half-sarcastic thought was that we might be going on a tour. I was kind of curious to see the facility, which I assumed was some kind of clinic for emergencies since we were so far from a real hospital.

Annoyed with the short notice but resigned to going, I grabbed the o.j. and corn muffin and shoved the rest of the basket inside my door with my foot.

"Hey." I turned at the call to find Miranda, looking abnormally plain in a black track suit, her hair pulled straight back into a ponytail. I figured I shouldn't tell her how the dark clothes really brought out the bags under her eyes. "Walk with me?" That she asked instead of demanding was an even bigger indicator that she must be feeling pretty low.

When I hesitated for just a second, my eyes shifting to Bliss's door, she was quick to inform me, "She's already gone. The *stars* were called up first, before anyone else was even awake. Now it's just us rejects."

The bigger the ego, the messier the fall, I thought. I hated to admit it, but the fire-breathing Miranda dragon of yesterday was actually preferable to this defeated blob.

"Snap out of it, Miranda," I ordered. "I'm definitely not walking with you if I have to listen to that garbage the whole way." I headed for the stairs, not sure if she'd follow.

She caught up with me at the door, if only to defend her side of the argument, and trailed me down the stairs. "Clio, in case you missed it, yesterday was a major smackdown." She blinked rapidly, looking for empathy.

"Why, because someone else got some attention?" I snorted, turning down the invitation to her pity party. "Who cares? There's always going to be someone who's better than you at something – that's life."

"It's not *my* life," she growled, and I was frankly glad to see some of her old self reemerging.

"Actually, it is while you're here, whether you like it or not." I lowered my voice as we went out the door to add, "You

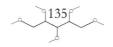

can spend the next couple weeks alone with your miserable self or you can get over it and keep your friends – your choice." I was harsher than I'd be with anybody else, but I felt like I knew her well enough by now to be sure she'd respond better to tough love than coddling.

Her responding "Hmph" confirmed that she was considering what I'd said, even if she wasn't prepared to concede yet.

Just as well, since my thoughts were now preoccupied with the ginormous health center that had come into view. It was now clear there were two very definite schools of thought in regard to the architecture around here. The main hall and dorm where we spent most of our time had been here forever and just rehabbed for us; those two buildings were constructed out of textured blocks the color of wet sand which, when used in a good design like at Tulane, could be attractive, but here were just stacked into plain square structures.

In complete contrast, the health center was done in the same strikingly modern style as the gym – all mirrored-blue glass – and was almost as large, which was the most curious part. *Why four floors of space with only a grand total of a hundred and fifty people on campus?* Even if we all got the swine flu at the same time, we still wouldn't need that many rooms.

I ran out of time to ponder that as Miranda and I were

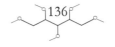

already approaching the front door, a line of our classmates already queuing up behind us. When I pushed firmly on the handleless door, however, it didn't budge. I leaned forward, cupping my hands around my eyes to try and see inside, but found only my own reflection.

"I think you have to use that," Miranda pointed to a scanner on our right, both her words and gesture making it clear that she'd wait for me to go first.

Closer examination revealed the device to be a fingerprint reader, so I carefully inserted my right index finger and waited. Within a second, an electronic voice announced, "Kaid, Calliope." The door opened and the voice simultaneously instructed, "Proceed."

Miranda started to follow me in, but a red light came to life overhead, accompanied by a short but distinctive alarm blast that stopped her in her tracks. In the ensuing pause, the glass slid silently between us, sending her back to the scanner and sealing me inside.

Okay, I noted, *only one person allowed through the door at a time.* I was curious, though, how the system had detected the second presence when she'd been barely a step behind me. *And so much for a place to run to in an emergency — you could bleed out trying to get in*, my cynical side commented. *You'd really be screwed if the emergency was a severed hand.*

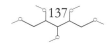

Without realizing it, I'd walked up to what appeared to be a reception desk. Sadly, the guy with the earpiece was about as receptive as the door.

"Proceed," he said, with only the slightest eye shift. Looked like his vocabulary was the same as the door's as well.

I followed his eye direction twenty feet or so to the left where another print scanner was mounted in the center of a wall of what looked to be elevator doors. When my scan triggered the opening of the third mirrored section, however, I found a short, stark hallway, ending in a standard-ish exam room.

Standard aside from the fact there was no equipment of any kind — just a flat, padded table for the patient and a long, empty countertop polished to a mirrored-shine. The fresh white paint and almost-blue halogen lights made the room feel much colder than it actually was — completely the opposite of my home doctor's. Dr. Missy Brightner always had music playing, tropical fish, fresh flowers — her office was very full of life. This place was full of...well, nothingness.

"Miss Kaid," came a sterile greeting from behind me.

Crap, my brain automatically reacted to the voice of Dr. Larson. I'd been hoping for a friendly lady doctor, had expected a flat but at least civil one, and had now tragically ended up with the absolute bottom of the personality barrel.

He finished entering something into what looked like an

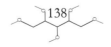

electronic clipboard. It was the size of an iPad, but not even half as thick. I wondered what he'd done to hit the tech jackpot. And how bad Janet and the others must've been to get stuck with the notepads.

He hit the last key, set the gizmo on the counter, then said, "Have a seat." When I hesitated for a second, he added, "On the table."

Thanks, I got that, I retorted inwardly. *Like there're any other options.*

I sat down obediently, finding the table to be conveniently set so that I didn't have to climb up onto it. As soon as my weight settled on the pad, however, the whole thing raised automatically until I was eye-level with the doctor.

Obviously the two types of buildings here fell at the opposite ends of the technology spectrum as well, from landlines at the other end of campus to all the fully-automated sensors here. I couldn't decide which of the two was more disconcerting.

"Am I supposed to lie down?" I asked, hoping the answer was *no*.

"Unnecessary," he said, his clipped answers starting to unnerve me. But I held my tongue and watched him push a button in the wall above the counter – the first on a panel of four that I now noticed for the first time. I realized that it wasn't really a button when out popped a capped syringe, which he removed

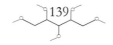

and pulled toward us, a good measure of plastic tubing maintaining its connection to the wall.

"Blood draw." With no words of comfort or warning about a pinch, he turned over my arm and jabbed in the needle. The collection tube filled quickly and he plucked it out of my arm, capped it, and returned it to its slot, where it readily retracted back into the panel.

Well, that's one way to do it, I supposed. *Should we call that the shock and awe technique?*

Before I'd even really wrapped my mind around the blood draw, he'd already moved on to step two. Dr. Larson voiced his next command, "Open your mouth," at the same time he pressed the second button, this time rewarded with a cotton swab in a plastic tube. Even faster than he'd been with the syringe, he swabbed my inner cheek, tucked the stick back into the tube, and shoved the tube back into its hole.

"Noninvasives," he said next, and I took it to mean he wasn't going to be breaking the skin from here on out, but I still didn't know what to expect. I was hugely relieved when he turned to his computer, tapped out a quick command on the screen, then held it up to reveal what looked like a regular eye chart. *Nice app,* I noted.

Once I'd read the letters to his satisfaction, he extracted a pair of ear buds from his lab coat pocket. "Audio," he explained,

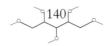

not wasting any words, although a "please" would've been good. I wordlessly inserted the tiny devices into my ears while he plugged the other end into his computer to begin what I assumed was going to be a hearing test. Luckily I'd done this before for the school nurse and knew to raise alternating hands when I heard the sounds, because he still wasn't offering instructions.

"Now I'm going to listen to your breathing," he said, holding out his palm. *Wow, a whole sentence,* I thought, careful not to touch him as I handed over the earpieces. I wasn't sure he'd had it in him.

I couldn't help but ask, "Your computer does that, too?"

"Of course not," he snapped and we returned to silent mode, which seemed to better serve both of us.

I took several deep breaths while he listened with the stethoscope he'd produced from his other pocket. Thankfully he did so through my shirt, as I had a feeling his hands would be even colder than his personality.

Done with that, he moved on to my favorite part of any physical exam – the karate-chop-to-the-knee test. When my lower leg flung out reflexively, I giggled hysterically because, as everyone knows, it's hysterical.

His sharp look made it clear that he did not share my sense of humor and he briefly entered another note into my electronic chart.

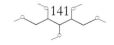

When he pulled out a wand like they use for airport security, I had to ask what it was for since it seemed like a foreign object in a medical facility.

"X-rays," he answered matter-of-factly and poised it over my head.

"Don't I need one of those heavy coats?" It was a tough call to decide whether or not to question Dr. All-Important, but TV doctors always seemed pretty concerned about radiation. I may have some messed-up chromosomes, but ending up with tumors and fins was a whole 'nother level.

"No," he answered, clearly not open to argument. He brought the wand down the front of my body in a sweeping motion all the way to my toes, then across the bottom of my feet and at a ninety degree angle behind my legs and up my backside. I really didn't see how he got a full scan with me in a sitting position and part of the table in the way but I wasn't about to say anything that could result in staying here longer.

"Done," he said with finality, but after checking his wristwatch he added, "Unless you have any questions," like he'd suddenly remembered the day in med school where they told him you were supposed to actually care about the patients.

I actually had about a million questions, but doubted he had the time or willingness to answer more than one, so I went with, "I don't understand why I had to come in – didn't you

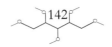

142

already get all this from my doctor?" We'd given blood samples and DNA swabs in our hometowns days before coming here, so I'd assumed those tests wouldn't need to be repeated.

"I find self-gathered data to be superior," he responded, pretty much like I'd expected him to.

"So you're personally examining all one hundred of us?" I decided if he'd answered the one, I'd keep rolling until he shut me down.

"All *ninety-five* subjects, yes," he clarified. "Beginning at oh-six-hundred hours with each exam taking eight minutes and allowing two minutes for room transfer, I'll be finished by twenty-two hundred this evening."

"No breaks?" I don't know why I even asked, since obviously robot-man would have no need to pee.

He didn't have to tell me I was cutting into "transfer time" – his narrowed eyes said it for him. I hopped off the table without waiting for it to lower me down and headed for the door. "Don't worry; I'll let myself out," I assured him, but he'd already gone through a passage on the opposite wall, presumably to see his next subject. *I mean, patient – semantics, right?*

Wow, I thought as I passed back through the lobby and then outside, dismissed by the electronic greeter even without a departing scan, *he should be working in a lab with dishes and tubes, not people.*

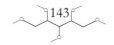

I looked around at the next group of kids waiting to be admitted, but didn't see anyone I recognized. I decided not to wait and see if Miranda would emerge in the next eight minutes and started back toward the dorm instead. I couldn't wait to call my mom to tell her about my strangest experience yet. It'd been almost a week since we'd talked, so today had better be the day we finally linked up; if this went on much longer, I was worried I'd start forgetting all the stuff I had to tell her.

Nah, I corrected my thought, *it'd be pretty hard to forget even a small part of this bizarre-ness.*

FIFTEEN

*S*mall surprise, but large annoyance – my call went straight to my mom's voice mail. Again. There was one bright spot, though – while I'd been out enduring the alien abduction exam, Janet had slipped the song lyrics I'd asked for under my door.

I pulled my journal out of the desk drawer, then flopped across my bed to start copying down the words. I flipped slowly through the hand-written pages, starting with *It's a Wonderful World* by Louis Armstrong – my mom's favorite song that she sang me to sleep with when I was a baby. I paused over Cowboy Mouth's *Take Me Back to New Orleans*, remembering being on my mom's last book tour, which lasted the entire summer, and just wanting to sleep in my own bed. The written pages finally ended with Copeland's *Strange and Unprepared* – the last entry I'd written the night before heading up here.

To whoever said "poetry is a dead art," I'd counter that it was, in fact, very much alive and well, just now found on shiny discs and satellite waves. I loved how the words to a song could perfectly capture my feelings about a moment, or a day, or a friend. I imagined someday putting together a massive compilation, like a sort of soundtrack of my life that I'd be able to listen to and relive all my memories.

After I'd finished entering the final refrain of the newest song – and making a mental note to find some Jamie Cullen to commemorate last night, now that the Internet seemed to be working again – I noticed Janet's handwriting at the bottom of the typed page. *Don't forget to look before you cannonball...,* she'd scrawled, alluding to the chorus printed above.

Should I tell her about Jack? I wondered. So far, I'd had to rely on divine intervention to overcome my stumbles, but she was decently young and cool; maybe she'd have some older-sister wisdom about how not to mess it up. *More importantly,* it suddenly dawned on me, *should I go to her with what I'd overheard on Sunday?*

No, my mental reaction was almost instantaneous. It was too soon to blur the mentor boundary with all that just yet. I had to wait and see what my friends thought of the news bulletin before I took it to the next level.

I returned to my pen and journal for some writing therapy. Thinking, re-thinking, and over-thinking had started

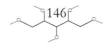

taking their toll on me, and the brainless-ness of copying lyrics was exactly what I needed to give my mind a break.

Before I knew it, I'd lost a whole hour, and I'd run out of time for the shower I really wanted to detox from the Larson Lab Experience. I settled for a quick change of clothes and an anti-bacterial gel rubdown over all my exposed parts to get rid of the heebie-jeebies before dinner.

Even in my rush, I noted how everyone I passed on my way across the courtyard was much more subdued than usual. Plenty of kids were still hanging out in the halls and sitting together outside, but without the normal laughing and fooling around, confirming that I wasn't the only one feeling off after the day's events.

But then came a pick-me-up like no other; I could hardly believe it when, crossing the great room, I was welcomed by the wondrous aroma of fried chicken. I practically skipped into the dining room with the anticipation of my all-time favorite dinner. My stomach jumped giddily when I saw that the chefs had once again proven themselves top-notch, putting out not only biscuits and potatoes with gravy, but also snappy green beans, not cafeteria-mush ones.

Bliss, Garrett, and Jack were already seated at our usual table, which allowed me to pretend I was shoveling food onto my tray in a rush to join them, not just out of sheer gluttony. I almost

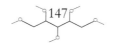

blew past the silverware stand, thinking, *Who needs a fork when you can use the chicken to scoop up the potatoes and eliminate the middle man?* If there weren't other people around, I might've dived into my plate face-first like a pie-eating champ, but Jack's presence in particular reminded me to maintain a basic level of decency.

After I sat down between Bliss and Jack, I glanced up to see Miranda distastefully picking her way, literally, around the salad bar. She was purposely not looking in our direction, so of course Garrett felt obliged to shout across the room, "Hey, M-cat! Don't pretend you don't see us! Pick your poison and get over here."

Bliss delivered an elbow to his ribs at the same time I hissed, "Don't poke the tiger, dummy!"

But, surprisingly enough, Miranda did make her way over to us. Of course, she also made a point of cramming herself between Jack and Garrett, acknowledging me with only the briefest glance, and letting her eyes pass over Bliss completely, as if hers were an empty chair.

Baby steps, I hoped, shifting my butt on the memory-foam seat cushion – a small comfort in the otherwise painfully awkward situation.

As usual, Garrett was the only one oblivious to the friction. He launched right into, "So how much did that suck, getting probed on the Mother Ship today?" Pausing for us to

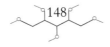

agree, he tipped back his Coke for a chug, only to have it knocked out of his hand by Miranda.

"Hey, I was drinking that!" He protested, watching the can spin to a stop a good ten feet away.

"You should thank me," she defended herself. "Carbonation promotes cellulite. I'm saving your shot at an *S.I.* cover."

"Where'd you read that?" Garrett asked, now more curious than irritated.

"A magazine," she retorted indignantly, not used to having her expertise called into question.

"Which one?" Jack chimed in, taking his own teasing stab at the angry wildcat.

"Who cares? It's true." She waved the boys off, done with both of them.

In the interest of group harmony, Garrett shrugged his shoulders and conceded, "It wasn't that good anyway." And not to be long derailed, he returned to his earlier topic. "So what'd you guys think of today's festivities?"

Here was my opening, so I decided to go for it before I lost my nerve. "Um, am I the only one who has some concerns about what's going on here?"

The words were barely out of my mouth when Garrett jumped in. "For real? Like today was the first time you noticed

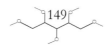

that Lurkin' Larson speaks Vulcan and Planet Janet doesn't orbit the same sun as the rest of us?"

I didn't respond right away, thrown off a bit by his observation. Not that any words from me would've been heard over Miranda's reaction, anyway.

"If you thought things were so off, why didn't you tell us?" Miranda, of course, was obviously unfamiliar with the concept of an oral filter.

"Dudes, it's the Army," Garrett replied, like it was a given. "It's not like they're gonna be cool."

"It's more than that." Bliss interrupted, turning to me with a sharp look and the order, "Tell them."

Secure in knowing that at least Bliss didn't think I was crazy, I related the conversation from the woods to the whole group. I let it all out in one big gush before I could chicken out, then caught my breath and waited for their reactions.

"Well, that's outstanding," Miranda grumbled first. "Everyone can see our cracks hanging out, but no one has the decency to tell us." Even though I didn't need her graphic metaphor in my head, I was grateful to hear that she didn't doubt what I'd overheard.

"What do you think they were talking about?" Garrett jumped on board beside her, and I felt guilty for initially doubting both of them.

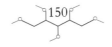

"Well, yesterday we saw what the stars can do," I started, hating to bring up the dividing issue between Bliss and Miranda, but it was the only logical starting place. "But that happened *after* I heard the people talking by the woods, so they must've meant something else."

"Everyone knows the jocks rock it," Garrett reminded us. "We're fast, we're light, we leap tall buildings in a single bound. Yes, we're the stuff legends are made of, my friends." He held up his hands as if to say, *What else can I say?* and tried to dim his grin to at least a pretend-modesty wattage.

"And we've got your opposites, density-wise," Jack put forward. "They even call themselves 'heavies' because they're like blocks. People go out of their way to avoid them, even if they don't know why."

"That's because they're all disturbed, not superhuman," Miranda threw in her biased opinion.

"Then there's your disappearing group," Jack went on as if she hadn't spoken. "What?" he asked when the rest of us looked at him blankly.

"Jack, besides the stars, none of us has been able to do anything." I gave him my most pointed look, hoping he'd get the hint and stop emphasizing how Bliss was so special in front of Miranda.

"Are you serious?" Jack looked confused by our

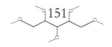

reactions. "Do you really not know what I'm talking about?" He finally said, pausing to search for the best words. He eventually decided to just throw it out there. "You vanish. All of you."

"What?" Bliss emerged for the first time from her low profile. "If that's true, how come none of us have seen it happen?"

"I have no idea, but believe it," he assured her. "I walked up to a field of sixty people, but then you did your thing and suddenly it was like I was all alone with Janet." To spare Miranda's feelings, he left out, *until the sparkling started.*

"That's what they said – the people I overheard," I said, making the connection out loud. "That maybe we couldn't actually see it, since we were all in the same state." Then I turned to Jack questioningly. "So you saw us disappear, like, instantly?"

"Not instantly," he corrected, "but, yeah, it was pretty fast. Kind of like a quick-fade photo in a slideshow." He still looked a little confused that he'd been the only one to see what'd happened.

And I found myself too overwhelmed to sort out my own tornado of feelings. On the one hand, I was thrilled with the knowledge that I could actually make myself invisible – *Get out of here!* But, on the flip side, I felt totally foolish for not even knowing I was doing it. And besides trying to wrap my head around those two things, I also still had to figure out why

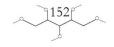

multiple other people had known these facts, but had been keeping them from us. I didn't want to, but I felt like I had to put my own self-reflection on hold to focus on the greater mission of finding out exactly who was up to what, and ASAP.

Then, all at once, everyone started bubbling over with questions, the gist of them all being: *Why did they bring us here?*

"And why did they work so hard to make everything so nice for us?" ever-innocent Bliss asked the follow-up.

"If they were just going to screw us, you mean?" Miranda asked, not worrying about winning the too-nice award. "To keep us fat and happy so we wouldn't ask these kinds of questions, obviously." I realized my fork was halfway to my mouth when she said this and I guiltily set it back down as she sounded the call to arms. "Let's stop whining and take them down."

Funny words coming from the girl who's been floating around the pity pool all day, I thought, but then there was nothing like a good fight to snap Miranda out of a funk. If they were smart, the Army would focus their recruiters on enlisting *her.*

While Miranda launched her crusade, Jack assumed the role of strategist. "Let's go over what we know," he began. "A secret military experiment creates a troop of super-kids. Years later, the Army finds out, feels guilty, and sets up a camp to bring everyone together for a summer of fun. When you listen to how hokey all that sounds, it seems ridiculous that we didn't suspect

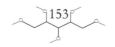

there was more to the story before now," he admonished. "Now the big question is: *Which of those dozen holes do we dig into first?*"

"I say we go straight for the big man," Garrett answered boldly. "Clark's gotta know everything that goes on here."

"We're supposed to confront him?" Bliss shivered at the thought.

"Not with suspicions and hearsay," I pointed out. "We need evidence."

"Looks like we need to search his office then," Jack said, taking the next logical step.

But Miranda was skeptical. "How do we get in?" she asked.

"The *how*'s all mine, what about the *when*?" Jack seemed to share none of her doubts.

"I vote we do it tonight." Garrett needed no convincing. "No time like the present, right?"

"I'm not so sure this is a good idea," Bliss held out.

Miranda took that as her cue to go full-force opposition. "It's the only idea," she said firmly. She may've been slightly placated with the discovery of her vanishing ability, but clearly her fur was still a bit ruffled by her star-less status.

"Okay, so it's tonight. Are we all going?" I pushed us forward to firm up the plan before I could think it down.

"No doubt!" Garrett rose to the role of cheer-master.

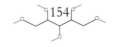

"Fun for the whole fam!"

"I'll get Clio and Miranda into the office," Jack began handing out parts. "The three of us should be able to do a good search. You two," he indicated Bliss and Garrett, "will run the block on the outside."

"I can't stop anyone!" A squeak burst from Bliss's petite hundred-pound frame.

"Not physically," Jack assured her. "You're going to use your dazzling ability to distract anyone who comes our way. I've seen you in action and, believe me, it's as effective as a body slam."

"So Miranda and I can get by Janet...," I began.

"...but Bliss can't," finished Miranda, happy to best her in one area.

"Don't sweat it; I'll pick you up." Garrett threw Bliss a wink.

"Sounds like we're on," Jack summed it up. "We hit Clark's office at midnight."

"Can we really do this?" Bliss still wasn't a hundred percent sold on the idea.

"Failure is not an option," Garrett admonished her in his most ominous voice. "Come on!" He addressed the table when he didn't get the desired reaction. "*Apollo 13*? Guys, you've gotta work with me here. I swear it's like I'm alone half the time...."

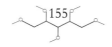

SIXTEEN

"Hello, Garrett's Angels!" Garrett called out appreciatively, while somehow managing to keep his voice low. Miranda and I walked up to the designated meeting spot on the shadowed side of the main building to see Jack and Bliss already waiting there, too.

"I'm thinking Covert-Op Tuesday should be an inker on our social calendar from now on," Garrett added, complimenting our all-black outfits of fitted long-sleeved tops and leggings.

Although the tight clothes may not have left much to the imagination, we'd chosen them out of necessity. Or so I thought, until Garrett said, "But it's not like you had to go all ninja when you're just going to *vanish*." He emphasized the last word with bugged-out eyes, "jazz" hands, and a game-show-host grin. *Hmm, hadn't thought of that.*

"What if they can't disappear tonight?" Jack defended our

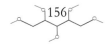

choice when we couldn't. "Or they can't keep it up as long as they need to?"

"Yeah, all that. What he said," Miranda was quick to grab the life ring, and Bliss and Garrett nodded in agreement with the logic. Jack flashed me a wink that would have been much appreciated at any other time, but now released a frenzy of butterflies in my already nervous stomach, just when he was supposed to be putting me more at ease.

"So why are you fools *not* in black?" Now that her decision had been justified, Miranda took a shot at everyone else.

"'Cuz if we get stopped for being out, we're *headed to the gym*," Garrett told her with an unspoken, *duh*. He and Jack had dressed the part in t-shirts and wind pants and their cover story was perfect, since the jocks were in and out of the gym at all hours.

Bliss had also gone couldn't-sleep-out-for-some-air casual in shorts and a top that probably could've doubled as pajamas. After giving her a once-over, I had to ask, "How'd you get out of the dorm?"

"Garrett jumped into that big tree by the building, then over to my window ledge," she answered, flushing like a rescued – and smitten – damsel. "I hung onto his neck and he carried me down the same way."

"I told you I had her," Garrett reminded us.

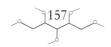

"You got lucky her window faces the back of the building, not the courtyard," Jack pointed out. He hadn't been as confident in Garrett's plan, but it'd all worked out and here we were. Next he turned his concern to me, "No problem getting out?"

"We didn't see a soul," I assured him. And it was a good thing we hadn't, because neither Miranda nor I was convinced the whole invisibility thing even worked yet. I told the others how we'd practiced in my room before making our move, but we still hadn't seen anything change in ourselves or in each other. Watching myself in the mirror, I'd thought for a split second I'd seen a waver in the air, like steam rising off summer pavement, but when I'd blinked, it was gone – clearly, my imagination was running in overdrive.

"Try again and I'll tell you if it's working," Jack suggested.

"Yeah," Garrett rocked up and down on the balls of his feet, anxious to see the special skill Jack had told him about.

Miranda and I looked at each other, took a deep breath, and focused on disappearing. Again, I saw and felt nothing, but knew we'd done it by Garrett's amazed, "Whoooaaa."

He reached one long arm toward what apparently looked to him like open space, and I had to take a quick step back before his paw landed right on my chest.

"Watch it," I complained, dropping the mind-chant and

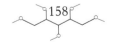

re-entering the visible world. Miranda laughed her way back beside me, a sound I was overwhelmingly glad to hear after the past two stormy days.

"You want to take a practice run, too?" Jack asked, turning to Bliss.

She nodded demurely, not thrilled about putting on a show, but also wanting to make sure she'd be able to perform on command if she had to.

And if Miranda and I thought *we'd* impressed him, Bliss's transformation totally blew Garrett's mind. "I think I'm...stupid-fied," he blurted, shaking his head. Five sets of laughter rang out, breaking the tension.

"Okay, freak show's over folks." Miranda was back to business. "Let's get going."

Jack went over the plan one last time. "Bliss will come in with us and wait in the hallway outside the door. She'll be our last line of defense, warning us if anyone shows up, then making a distraction so we can get out." He looked directly into her eyes to remind her, "But it's probably not going to come down to that. Garrett's got a good sense of who's out and when, and this is a pretty dead time."

Garrett reached around to pat himself on the back for the inadvertent recon before restating his own role in the mission. "I'll knock on the window if anyone's headed your way; one tap

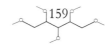

159

for maybe, so you can let Bliss know to be ready, or two for *GON*," he howled like a cartoon hillbilly. "That's short for Get Out Now," he explained.

"But even if you could reach the window from the ground, *which you can't*, you'll be seen," I pointed out, wondering if I was the only one who thought he was delusional.

"You don't have to be invisible when you're in a place nobody's gonna look." He grinned and puffed out his chest like a little kid's Halloween costume, then leapt into the tree at the corner whose thick limbs stretched to just above Colonel Clark's office window. The lowest branch had to be ten feet up, but he landed solidly onto it, as agilely as a jaguar.

This is ridiculous, I said to myself. *Vanishing, sparkling, and now literally leaping and bounding like Superman?* Eventually I might grow accustomed to seeing my friends perform these crazy feats, but for now I was floored.

Jack used his pointer finger first to shoot Garrett, now camouflaged by the conveniently-placed greenery, a farewell salute, then to signal the rest of us to follow him in. Miranda and I took the outside flanks, pretty sure that our invisibility would not be able to mask the others, but figuring it couldn't hurt either.

We needn't have worried. We didn't see or hear a thing as we skirted the edge of the quiet courtyard and darted through the

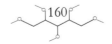

door into the equally deserted building. Clark's office was not far in, and we were in front of his door in moments.

"Are you sure there's nobody here at night?" Bliss asked, seemingly even more nervous because of the oppressive silence.

"All staff members who aren't mentors on one of our wings live in quarters on the first floor at the back of the dorm," Jack told her again. "They always go straight back there after dinner, probably to talk about us. And the cleaning crew was done by ten." How he could keep his patience when dealing with her near-panic was beyond me; I loved Bliss to death, but the constant worrying was exasperating even me.

"How do we get in?" I asked Jack, trying to focus on our actual obstacles, not ones we hadn't run into yet.

Jack put his hand on the knob and smiled back at me. "Clark says he's got an open-door policy, so I'm thinking we can just walk right in." When the knob actually turned in his hand and the door swung open, however, he was as startled as the rest of us. "Who knew that would work?" he said, and I cheered inwardly at what had to be a good sign.

Miranda and I scooted by him to start searching while he settled Bliss, physically and mentally. He put both hands on her shoulders to guide her into position about six feet away and, handing her a brick paver I hadn't seen him grab from the edge of the path, told her, "Here's your spot. If anyone comes, *which they won't*, drop this on the floor to signal us, then do your thing." She nodded mutely as he moved into the office, leaving the door slightly cracked behind him.

Once inside, he flicked on a mini-maglite to give me enough light to look through the desk drawers. Miranda quickly got to work on the bookshelves, feeling around and behind all the military manuals for anything that may be hidden there.

"Uh-oh," I said when I found the first drawer locked. I looked underneath to see not just a regular keyhole, but a serious-looking dead-bolt holding it shut from the side. There was obviously something worth seeing in there, *but how to get at it?*

Undeterred, Jack cracked, "Did you think you just brought me along for my good looks?" *Because that would be a bad reason?* I wondered.

He pulled a tiny pick out of his pocket and in a matter of seconds the drawer slid open toward me. "My dad's Special Forces," he explained with a shrug. "You should see what my older sisters can do – they've had a couple more years of at-home training than I have." *Good to know.*

In unspoken agreement, I moved to start with the files at the front end, Jack at the back. "We'll meet in the middle like Lady and the Tramp with the spaghetti," I said, the mortifying comparison out of my mouth before I could stop it. "But way less messy," I added, feeling my face go marinara.

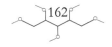

Just stop talking, I silently reprimanded before I embarrassed myself any further.

I pulled out the first thick file and flopped it open on top of the desk, hoping to find something useful to change the topic to. "These are letters he wrote to like every officer asking to be assigned to this post," I summarized for the others, flipping through sheet after sheet of almost exactly the same one. At first I thought they must be copies, but then I saw that each page had a different date. "And they go back a long, long way," I gulped, putting it together. "As in *before* there was even a post here to fill."

"Well that doesn't make sense," Miranda responded without turning from her own search area. "Why would he want to come here so bad? They don't even have a day spa."

"Didn't you hear me?" I tried again. "Some of these letters go back to when there was no *here* at all."

"But there's always been a here," she disagreed, looking up at the ceiling. "See? Those tiles are totally asbestos, and the *dinosaurs* banned that stuff."

"Okay, before there was an *us* then," I clarified, frustrated, just wanting her to see past the little shadows to the big shadiness of the secret.

"I'm with you," Jack chimed in, and I wondered why it'd taken him so long to say so. I didn't feel any better when I got

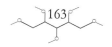

the answer.

"I think I've got something," he said, putting another fat manila folder on top of mine. He pointed to the label *CGK* and said, "You might want to take a look at this."

It took me a second to realize the letters weren't some secret code, but *my initials*. And I could tell by the way Jack was biting down hard on his lower lip that he'd figured out the same thing.

He considerately turned away to keep digging through the file drawer so that I could have some privacy to check out the shockingly thick file on me.

Nausea climbed up my throat, the acidy taste in my mouth forcing me into the colonel's chair. I pulled the folder onto my lap and shakily leafed past my birth certificate, doctor's records, grade-school photos and report cards, a copy of my driver's license exam and even my SATs – the whole test, not just the results. There were also lots of cryptic, hand-written notes, saying things like "KRDO weather" and "quartermaster."

But none of that prepared me for the contents of the envelope at the very bottom of the pile. I shook out its contents and dozens of photos spilled onto my lap – candid shots of me from when I was little right up until, well, *now*, I realized, picking up one that'd been taken on the tarmac of Louis Armstrong International as I boarded the plane with Lieutenant Graham.

I dropped the picture as if it'd bitten me and put my hand over my mouth. *What did this mean? Colonel Clark had been stalking me?* Either that, or he'd paid someone else to. And my gut told me it was more than just brotherly loyalty to my dad. *Somewhat shady* was speedily becoming *seriously sinister.*

"More bad news." Jack said, and I was glad for the distraction. He hauled out yet another of the olive green folders that I was really starting to detest. "I've got campus plans here dating back over a year – well before the 'secret informant' came forward about the experiment. And there're more sketches behind that with no dates, but the notes on them are in Clark's handwriting."

"So he *knew*," Miranda said, concluding her search and coming over to join us. "Clark knew even before the Army did."

I looked down at the pile of snapshots in my lap and whispered, "I'm pretty sure he knew all along."

"What do you mean?" Miranda asked, leaning over to see what I was talking about.

Bang! The sound of the paver hitting the floor resounded from the hallway. Miranda was closest to the door, but Jack rushed past her to check on Bliss. Miranda and I exchanged a frozen look before I caught a glimpse through the crack Jack'd opened in the door to see Bliss shaking her head guiltily.

"False alarm," she whispered. "It just slipped out of my

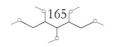

hand."

Before Miranda could cue up a lecture on clumsiness, Jack came back around the desk and started closing up the incriminating files and dropping them back into their slots. "We should get out of here anyway," he said, pausing with his hand on the back of my chair to look into my eyes before removing the stack on my lap.

"Right," I agreed, "okay." I hoped he could tell I meant that *I* was okay, too. *Okay enough to get out of this room, anyway.*

Keeping his voice low as he reengaged the locks and herded me toward Miranda and the door, he went on, "We've seen enough to know our suspicions are right on. Let's not press our luck tonight."

SEVENTEEN

When the five of us reconvened first thing the next morning at the outermost bench of the courtyard, we all looked the worse for wear. After filling Garrett and Bliss in on what we'd found in Clark's office, then trying out a million different conspiracy theories that turned my stomach over and over, we'd only finally gone back to our rooms just before sun-up.

I didn't know what the others had done for the couple of hours we were apart, but I'd spent them pacing back and forth across my room, thinking back and forth across my *life* to all the times that I now knew had been haunted by an uninvited guest. I didn't think calling my mom at two, or three, or four a.m. California time was the best choice, so I'd had to stick with mumbling to myself until the clock reached a reasonable enough hour that I could "get up" and go out.

And now here we sat – a virtual zombie movie cast, each

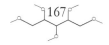

with deep under-eye circles and a death-like grip on a pick-me-up drink. It looked like Garrett'd been traumatized enough by the Coke smackdown yesterday to trade in his wake-up soda for the classic standard o.j. like Jack. I was just thankful the Starbucks had oatmeal, because I needed the warm goop to anchor my stomach.

Miranda showed up last with two cups of green tea, the second being a peace offering for Bliss. Although the gesture would've been more appreciated if she'd actually brought something Bliss liked – some thick and syrupy concoction, ultimately topped off with whipped cream. But she was Miranda, after all, so I had to give her credit for the attempt. Mostly, I was just relieved to have the group dynamic stable again when everything else seemed to be crumbling around us.

Besides sitting as far off the beaten path as possible without actually sneaking off somewhere and arousing suspicion, we were also benefiting from the cooler-than-average day. The cloudy gray sky not only reflected our somber mood, but the threat of rain was also keeping most everybody else inside, making this our best chance to talk openly without much risk of being overheard.

Miranda and Garrett were seated on opposite ends of the bench with Bliss between them, trying to shrink into herself as the two Titans engaged in the first skirmish of the day.

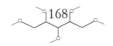

"Did you wash that?" Miranda disdainfully eyeballed the banana Garrett was peeling.

"To get off what? Monkey pee?" he retorted, biting off a huge chunk just to goad her.

"Insecticides, fungicides, nematicides...," Miranda rambled on and I realized that if she didn't lay off the "cides" she was going to end up a victim of friend-icide. And that was the best-case scenario.

"Seriously? With everything else we've got going on – *that's* what you're worried about?" Garrett put her in check.

Bliss remained as silent as a small child in the middle of a custody battle. She rubbed her temples, preferring to suffer the headache they were giving her rather than speak up and risk angering Miranda now that they were finally back on speaking terms.

While waiting for the skirmish to die down, I took the opportunity to lean my head on Jack's shoulder. We were lounging on the grass, leaning back on our elbows with our legs stretched out in front of us, facing the bench trio. I was glad for the chance to be close to him, not just because we hadn't had any alone-time since our constellation date, but more for the solidness of him and the calming effect he had on me. Without him to ground me, I'd surely be pacing a path across the grass like I'd almost worn through my floor in the early hours of the

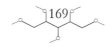

morning.

"When you grow a third eye, don't come crying to me," Miranda warned, having to have the final word.

"Hey, guys," I interrupted, leaning forward to get their attention. "Worse things than that may be in store for us if we don't figure out what's going on around here." Both litigants immediately stopped arguing in concession of my point, making me feel a bit foolish for thinking about Jack instead of our real problem.

"So let's go over everything we know," Jack, as always, directed the discussion.

Miranda wasted no time presenting her recap of the office findings. "We know that Clark's a freak who knew about C9x all along, stalked Clio her entire life, then designed this whack circus and set himself up as ringmaster."

Talking about Colonel Clark made me realize for the first time that I hadn't seen him hanging around lately like he had those first few days. When I shared my observation with the group, Bliss added, "And why hasn't he been at our group sessions? Isn't seeing our – well, Clio's – new ability the whole reason he's here?"

"Well, we know there's video," Garrett reminded us. "Guess the old dude likes to get his rocks off in the comfort of his own digs." He finished with a little *bow-chick-a-bow-wow* beatbox tribute to vintage adult cinema.

"Geriatric Perv," Miranda spat, actually happy to not be the focus of someone's attention for once.

"Enough," Jack stopped them. "Nothing in that file suggested that he had any kind of...," he paused to search for the most PC term, finally settling on "crush." He put his hand on my knee as he finished, the warmth of his hand flooding my entire body with reassurance – an intense reaction to someone I'd known only a week, but could now see I'd needed my whole life.

"Yeah," I agreed, not just because I wanted it to be true, but because instinct told me that he was right. "It feels more *parental*, with the report cards and all. I just don't get the why of it."

"Maybe we're overcomplicating that part," Bliss suggested, wanting nothing more than to lessen the evil at work. "What if it's just that he knew about the experiment and he had to track *someone*, so he picked someone he knew – his friend's daughter."

While the rest of us took a minute to turn over that possibility, Jack brought up a second topic. "Let's come back to the *why* after we get a better grasp on the *what* – as in, what we've seen going on here that's not legit."

"I'm not so down with being confined to campus," Garrett made the first point, adding, "And them not letting

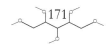

171

anyone else in."

"For our own safety and security – ha!" Miranda *Amen*-ed the complaint.

"I'm not real happy that we can't get online." I smiled to hear that, while the rest of us would've said "pissed," our sweet Bliss was merely "not happy." She complained, "They didn't tell us we'd be cut off like that."

"Like I said, they gave us everything else we could've asked for so that we wouldn't realize what we were missing," Miranda growled, her voice betraying that having been duped for even a short time had rattled her cage.

"I don't get how everyone keeps saying the server is down or there's no connection or whatever, but Janet could get online and you, too, right?" I looked to Jack for confirmation.

"Now that you mention it…," he said, and I saw the puzzle pieces arranging themselves in his brain. "I tried a bunch of searches and just got an error message about the server. Then I went to take a shower, and when I came back and looked up the same stuff again, I got through to some pages."

I was about to say, *So the Internet must have been working for at least a short time*, but he wasn't done yet.

"What's funny is that all the pages I got to were cached articles – no active screens. Since it was all research stuff, I didn't think anything of it until now." He shook his head, clearly

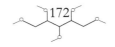

disappointed in himself, and I covered his hand with mine in an attempt to give back some of the reassurance he'd shared with me.

Then I brought up my biggest frustration. "We haven't even talked about the phones yet."

"Yeah, what's up with that?" Garrett agreed, even more indignant than I was. "I haven't had a single jingle from my bros or…ladies." He checked himself just in time.

"My parents are on a cruise," Miranda chimed in. "I just figured when all my calls went straight to voice mail, they didn't have reception on the ship." It was dawning on all of us at the same time that *all* of our families couldn't possibly be too busy cruising, commanding troops, and signing books to return even one of our calls. We were even more isolated than we'd thought.

As that realization sunk in, and I was starting to feel like things couldn't get any bleaker, I was not cheered by the appearance of our least favorite hall-mate, Alexis.

"Um, I didn't mean to eavesdrop…," she began, coming to a stop right beside me. But my *yeah, right* gut reaction to her denial was softened when I looked up into her face. Her expression wasn't full of delight in having caught us up to no good like I'd expected, but a mixture of curiosity and concern. Enough to convince us all to hold our tongues and listen to what she had to say at least.

"You said the phones aren't working?" she asked.

"How could you *not* know that?" Miranda's brief bout of tolerance had apparently passed.

"I haven't made any calls," Alexis replied, as if that were normal behavior for a teenage girl.

"What about your parents?" Bliss couldn't comprehend Alexis not having at least called home when it was killing her that she hadn't spoken to her dad in a week.

"My parents died last year," she answered, mostly matter-of-factly, but a tiny crack in her voice betrayed the emotion behind the words. "So no, nobody to call really."

"Who looks out for you?" Jack asked, falling into protector-mode.

"Me," she said simply. "I got emancipated after the accident and since I had an early acceptance to Juilliard, the lawyer sold the house, set up a trust for my tuition, and I left D.C. to move into student housing in New York in time for fall semester." Her tone stayed even, not emboldened by pride in the bravery and strength she must've needed to get through that.

"You must be so lonely. Do you have a roommate at school?" I asked, hopefully not nosily. Even though I only had the one-person support team of my mom at home, to be totally and completely alone seemed unbearable to me.

"Nah, I've got a single. People tend to give me a lot of

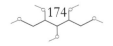

space." Alexis tried to laugh it off but the rest of us squirmed with embarrassment at how we'd done exactly that – kept our distance from her. Whether we'd turned away from her defensive demeanor or reacted subconsciously to what Jack had been trying to tell us was the heavies' blocking ability, it didn't really matter. We should've tried harder to break through her barrier and get to know her and I, for one, now felt like a major jerk.

No more comfortable than the rest of us with the awkward pause, Alexis returned to our communication situation. "Do any of you have your cell on you?"

Jack readily produced his and handed it over.

"You don't have one?" Miranda asked in disbelief, and I shot her a silencing glare. By the way she quickly turned her gaze to her shoes, I could tell she wasn't trying to be mean, she just hadn't been thinking.

Alexis ignored the question – out of politeness and not disgust, I hoped – as her thumbs raced back and forth across the keypad of Jack's phone. "Good, it's unlocked; we're not trapped by a SIM card," she mumbled to herself, then noticed we were all watching her expectantly. "That's what locks you in to only one provider, one signal. Anyway, I think they're just using a different GSM network here that your phones don't recognize."

"It's not just no bars?" Garrett only knew as much about how his phone worked as he'd seen in commercials.

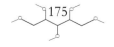

"No, there's an eco-tower right there, built to blend in." I followed her pointer finger to the woods and could just pick out the fake tree amongst the real ones. "Since we can see there's some kind of service out here, my guess is that the Army, being the Army, has a separate network from the phone companies. I bet they're also running on a less-used frequency, like the 850 band instead of the 900. Sorry, I'm kind of a techie," she apologized, returning the phone to Jack.

He, however, wasn't ready to take it back. "Can we get our phones onto that frequency or signal or whatever it is?"

"Probably. GSM's security level's not high – they just use a PSK to authentic users." She paused, then expanded the term for us, "Pre-shared key. Basically a password. So if I can establish what frequency they're on, then figure out the password for their network, I should be able to reset this phone and voila – you've got service."

"You can do that?" Garrett couldn't have been more impressed if she'd hit a grand slam.

"It'll take some time, but yeah, I think so," Alexis nodded, not Garrett-cocky, but more confident in herself than I'd ever seen her. Maybe our including her had helped break through her wall a little.

"What about the Internet?" Bliss was dying to get back to her Facebook page. "They're blocking that somehow, too."

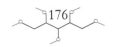

Jack tried to explain the computer issue to Alexis. "You can log onto the home page they've set up here, but if you try to go anywhere else, the server won't connect. And what's even weirder is that if you wait and try again later, you can get cached pages related to your subject."

"It's like the computer saves your search, runs it when you're gone, and gives you back what it's decided you should have," I thought aloud, not caring if it sounded far-fetched. *Really, these days pretty much all the impossibles were looking to be not only possible, but probable.*

"Like the landlines in our rooms," Jack piggy-backed onto my thought with another connection of his own. "We think we're getting to our parents' voice mails, but what if those are 'cached,' too? Recordings that don't really go anywhere."

"So you're thinking there's some kind of a server bank that all campus communications are being routed to," Alexis summarized.

"Is that possible?" Miranda had one-eightied from intense dislike of Alexis to now total faith in her knowledge.

"Definitely," Alexis confirmed, then added, "Unfortunately."

"That's why they made sure we all called home that first night." It suddenly dawned on me. "They waited until the next day to turn off the system *after* we'd all used it and assumed it

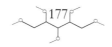

worked normally."

"Could it be working both ways?" Bliss was busy making her own frightened connections. "Like, our parents are leaving us messages and just thinking we're too busy to call them back?"

"Sure," Alexis said, then seeing how she'd confirmed Bliss's fears, quickly tried to do damage control. "But now I've got Jack's phone, he'll get me his laptop before group, and I'll figure it all out." And her steady calm had me believing she could.

"I'm going to go with you today and see if I can get a better feel for your group since none of us really know any of them," Jack said, standing up to follow Alexis, but not forgetting to offer me a hand up, too. "I seem to have free reign to drift around and try to *find myself*, after all," he added, words I found so ironic, as he was one of the most "found" people I'd ever known.

"We're just supposed to go to group and act like nothing's wrong?" Bliss fretted, terrible at lying, pretending, and hiding her feelings.

"We have to," Miranda told her, softening the order by taking Bliss's hand.

"Together," I added, taking Bliss's other hand in my own. In turn, we each met the eyes of the others, verifying our solidarity before temporarily disbanding. *Yes,* I thought, pausing to give myself a little reassurance, too, *the one thing we can be sure of is each other.*

EIGHTEEN

*B*y some miracle, we made it through our group session without any kind of crack, slip, or full-on breakdown. It helped that Janet was really hitting her stride as commander of our special vanishing and sparkling brigade, coming up with different things for us to do besides stand around and meditate. Of course, she had a lot of material to work with now that we could *do* more than stand around and meditate.

Ironically, the exercise she'd come up with today was to see if any of us could conceal another person under our cloak of invisibility. The result turned out to be *not*, which was pretty much the same conclusion Bliss and I had come to in the dorm-room trials we'd run last night as part of our mission decompression. Janet also had the stars attempt to mask a second person – an idea we *hadn't* thought of. And it sort of worked, because the witnesses were so completely blinded by the star that they couldn't see the person next to her, either.

The bonus of the mixed-ability activity was that we all worked as one big group – stars and vanishers together – allowing Miranda and I to stay close to Bliss and help her keep it together.

At break time, the three of us weren't really hungry, but we followed the rest of the kids toward the dining hall just for something to do. The more we could avoid sitting around worrying about what Alexis was doing and Colonel Clark was thinking, the better for all of us – Bliss in particular.

"Well, you got through group okay," I congratulated her, as she, Miranda, and I crossed the courtyard. Even though we hung a decent enough distance back from the crowd, I deliberately avoided the other looming subject.

"Yeah," she agreed. "I'm just glad Janet treats us like our abilities are normal, almost, not like we're freaks. That takes a lot of the pressure off."

"And Alexis has the phone and the laptop, so hopefully we'll get some good news soon," Miranda chirped. I appreciated her perkiness, but really wished she'd taken my cue and stuck to less sensitive subjects. She read my raised-eyebrow signal and diverted, "Hey, I won't even rag on you if you want to get a hot dog for lunch."

"Seriously?" Bliss stopped to question the offer that

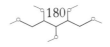

sounded way too good to be true.

And it was.

"Okay, you're right – I can't let you do that," Miranda admitted. "But it's for your own good! Don't you know what they put in those things?"

I will never complain about my mother's nagging again, I thought to myself. *She's got nothing on this girl.*

Just then, Miranda caught my eye over Bliss's head and winked, letting me know that this particular lecture was purely to refocus Bliss's mind. And it was working. Funny how even though my new friend could claw her way out to the tip of my last nerve, she could let go just as easily. The more I got to know her, the more substance I saw in her to work with.

Suddenly Garrett appeared around the far side of the dorm, having run up the path from the gym. "Clark's on the path down by the gym!" he informed us excitedly as Jack caught up to him.

"Okay?" I asked leadingly, not seeing where he was going with this.

"You said yourself that we haven't seen him around lately, especially alone. Here's our shot." His explanation was still somewhat cryptic.

"Shot at what?" Miranda asked for more clarification, too.

"To get our questions answered," Jack said, trying to

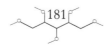

181

lasso all of our minds together.

"No way!" Distracted Bliss morphed back into frightened Bliss with a vengeance.

"Let's go," Miranda said, stepping forward as Bliss backed up. Once she had a mission, it was take no prisoners.

I could see that the others were anxious to move, too, but I also knew it was up to me to calm and convince our weakest soldier. "Bliss, there's five of us and only one of him. Plus, all we're going to do is ask a few questions." I stopped short of finishing with, *What's the worst that could happen?*, knowing that she could offer me many more options than I wanted to consider right now.

She didn't look fully convinced, but she did fall in line with the group as we reversed direction and headed back the way the guys had come. Garrett took the lead with Miranda at his right flank, while I guided Bliss behind them with a gentle but firm hand on her elbow so she couldn't bolt. Jack brought up the rear, making sure no one noticed our furtive departure. We may not know what we were doing, but we knew we didn't want an audience to watch us do it.

It took only a minute to get there, but when we reached the place where they'd spotted Colonel Clark, there was nobody to be found. Looking around, I realized we were at the exact spot where I'd overheard the ominous conversation three days ago.

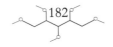

Sure that it couldn't be a coincidence, my eyes moved off the path to where I'd stretched out undetected that day.

And that's when he came into view – shaded by the edge of the woods with his back against the trunk of a tree. He had his knees pulled up to his chest, his fingers laced in a bridge on top, and his eyes closed, making him seem very exposed. He opened his eyes at our not-so-stealth approach, offering a genuine smile when he saw who it was. Even though he looked exhausted and very far from diabolical, I resolved to keep my wall up. I wanted to smile back, but with what we did – and didn't – know, we couldn't afford to trust anyone at this point, let alone him.

Jack spoke first. "Colonel Clark, we need to ask you some questions, sir." His genial tone would hopefully result in some answers for us.

"Absolutely. Like I've said from day one, I'm always available," the colonel said, rising to his feet without unclasping his hands to pull himself up. He may be dad-age, but he had some seriously strong quads. In that one movement, he went from vulnerable to imposing and I no longer felt any confidence in our plan to confront him.

Catching the same vibe, no one spoke right away, and he looked into each of our faces in turn. When his eyes finally came to rest on me, he directed, "Calliope?"

I should've known he'd single me out. And now it'd be

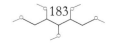

up to me to ask the questions. I took a deep breath, not sure where to start. I hadn't been one hundred percent behind this plan from the beginning, and was definitely not prepared to take the lead, but it was too late to back out now.

"Colonel Clark," I began, addressing him by full title, not only to be respectful, but really to buy myself an extra minute to sort out my words. This was certainly not the time to let my mouth run without a filter. "We know there's more going on here than we've been told," I said, deciding to keep it somewhat vague and see what he'd admit without prompting.

"Yes, I knew better than to underestimate the intuition of John Kaid's daughter," he acquiesced much too easily. The possibilities as I saw them were: one, he was ready to give it all up – *doubtful*; two, he still didn't know what we were talking about – *hard to believe, but possible*; or three, he'd seen this coming and had his own plan of attack – *the absolute worst option.*

"Don't do that," I said through gritted teeth, my hands clenching involuntarily at my sides. "Do not play the dead-dad card." No matter what his strategy, I wanted him to see me as a person, not just the child of an old friend. "Just tell us what you know. Tell us why we're really here." I saw that my friends' reactions ranged from a proud nod by Garrett to the shocked recoil of Bliss.

When Colonel Clark started blinking rapidly and looking

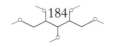

around again as if he wasn't sure how to answer, Miranda lost her patience. "Listen, Clark, we've seen your files. We know that you've been in on C9x from day one and you're gonna start spilling. Now."

"Yes, partly," he replied as ordered, surprising me. None of us had actually expected him to admit any wrong-doing, and the shock of it kept us quiet as he went on.

"I have known about the experiment much longer than I let on," he began, seeming almost relieved to unload the burden, "but I had to keep quiet until I was sure all of you would be taken care of."

"Taken care of?" Bliss squeaked. "As in *eliminated?*"

"Of course not!" he denied adamantly. "Everything I've done, I've done to *protect* you!" I noted that once again his words seemed directed at me.

But Jack, not about to let this become a one-on-one, moved to my side and asked, "Protect us from what, sir? The truth?"

"I had to protect you since I couldn't save the others who found out too much!" The colonel responded, his voice and his anger rising in unison. Then he stopped abruptly, checking himself so as not to risk drawing attention to us.

"There is no *too much.*" Unable to sit still any longer, Garrett took his turn as point person. "We get it all – from the

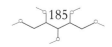
185

beginning."

My earlier surprise at his willingness to talk was nothing compared to the shock I felt as the colonel started to answer Garrett's demand.

"I found out about Dr. Heigl's experiment shortly after all of you were born," he started, going all the way back to the beginning. I fought to chamber my disbelief so I could absorb what was, in actuality, the story of us.

"I was a field medic in the Gulf," the colonel continued, "and when I got back stateside after the war, I was assigned to the lab at Detrick. I thought I'd be doing research, *helping people*, but Dr. Heigl treated me like a janitor. He had me clean his lab and do his grunt work without ever letting me see or touch anything significant. After awhile, he either forgot I was even there, or got a little cocky, because one night he left his journal behind. I'd never once seen it off his person. My intuition told me to look inside, so I did."

"What did it say?" Bliss leaned forward, as enrapt as a kid listening to ghost stories around a campfire.

"He'd made notes on everything – names, dates, how he'd administered the drug…," Colonel Clark stopped and squeezed his eyes shut at the painful memory, as if turning away from a gory movie scene. "Before that, I'd just thought he was a pompous jerk. But that's when I learned he was truly evil."

"How did he do it?" Jack cut in. "No one's ever explained that part to us."

"Oh, he was a clever man," Colonel Clark snorted derisively. "He put his little concoction in prenatal vitamins. The women unknowingly drugged *themselves*." The revelation hung in the air like a noose.

"Too many loose threads in that plan, sir," Jack pointed out after mulling it over for a minute. "How'd he know the vitamins wouldn't just sit on the pharmacy shelf? Or that the women who bought them would take them? Plus a hundred kids born within weeks of each other – how could he be sure of the timing? How could one man, without involving anyone else, possibly ensure that one hundred pregnant Army wives across the country took the same vitamins?"

Colonel Clark took the questions in order, one by one. "You don't get to be Chief Medical Officer of the United States Army by accident. He'd planned his experiment for years, waiting until the end of the Gulf War to implement it when all the troops were coming home and there were a lot of…conjugal reunions. The surge in pregnancies gave him such a large pool of test subjects that he was able to keep them spread out, choosing only one or two women at smaller bases and no more than five at the largest. That way, if anything unusual happened with the pregnancies or births, there'd be nothing to connect them to each

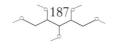
187

other, or to him. And he had the perfect fall-guy in his pocket – the war itself. Any genetic abnormalities could easily be blamed on Middle East toxins picked up by the fathers and passed on in their DNA."

"He knew he may only have one shot at it," he continued, making me feel like I was watching a bad infomercial – *But wait, there's more!* I wasn't sure how much more I could take, but I knew we might only get one shot, too.

"He noted that the drug had to be started during the first trimester to have any effect, otherwise the fetal tissues were too developed. So he worked quickly, managing to visit twenty-six bases over only ten weeks; that's why you were all born so close together."

I tried to digest this new piece of information. Obviously, I'd known we were all juniors in high school, but I hadn't asked anyone their actual birthdate. I briefly wondered if there were any other leap-day babies like me, then snapped back to the topic at hand.

Miranda hadn't lost focus for a second. "Seriously?" she interrupted, predictably finding the story a bit fishy. "Like there's just one baby doctor for the whole Army?"

"Of course not," Colonel Clark agreed. "He wasn't any of the mothers' doctors; that's why his rank was so essential to his experiment's success. He traveled from base to base under the

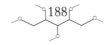

guise of routine inspections. On his 'rounds,' he'd identify newly pregnant women coming in for their check-ups and personally hand them a bottle of the tainted pills, making sure to emphasize their importance to the baby's health."

This time, before Miranda could pick at another snag in the story, he jumped ahead of her. "Yes, he knew there was a risk that some may not be taken, which is why he approached a hundred women. He wrote in his journal that he hoped *half* would comply. Once he'd handed off the pills, he pulled the women's files and tracked them through their pharmacies to see who refilled the vitamins after sixty days, indicating they'd taken the initial supply. Even he was shocked that all one hundred of his subjects ended up taking the pills. I guess he underestimated what good rule-followers they were."

This is crazy, my mind reeled, unable to take it all in. I felt like my brain was going to overheat until smoke started coming out of my ears like Frankenstein's monster. Except that this mad scientist story was even more unbelievable than Mary Shelley's. Demented Dr. Heigl had seemed to've thought through every detail.

No, not every one, I corrected myself. *Colonel Clark figured it out. And kept it to himself.*

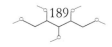

NINETEEN

"Why didn't you tell someone?" I demanded, fury and tears surging up in me at the same time.

"I did!" the colonel shot back indignantly, tears welling up in his eyes now, too. "I told the one man I knew I could trust with my life," he said softly, guiltily, and when he looked away, I realized what he was saying.

To keep from doubling over, I grabbed hold of Jack's steady shoulder. He immediately slipped his arm around my waist for support before asking the follow-up question that I couldn't. "John Kaid's death wasn't really an accident, was it?"

Colonel Clark shook his head ruefully. "I called him out in Colorado, where he was stationed, and told him what I'd found out. He dropped the phone and took off for the base right then." His gaze drifted off to the distance as he recalled that fateful night. "The official report said that he must've taken one of the curves down the mountain too fast and lost control of his motorcycle in the rain. But I knew." He turned to look me straight in the eye as he finished, "As soon as I heard, I knew what'd happened."

The first thought that jumped into my mind was, *My whole life is a lie. Nothing is real; nothing ever was real. Not me, not my body, not even before I was born.* Now it turned out that the little I'd known about my dad wasn't true either. And there was still one other person completely in the dark.

"How could you not tell my mom?" I practically shrieked, but I couldn't help myself.

"How could I *tell* her?" he responded, looking equally distraught. "How could I put you both in that kind of danger? You were John's whole world and, because of me, he was dead. I wouldn't let them get you, too." His tears finally spilled over, a deluge of sixteen-year-old guilt.

"So you did *nothing?*" Action-minded Garrett was unfamiliar with that concept.

"No," the colonel corrected Garrett, "I confronted Heigl, and he made it clear that he not only had no intention of turning himself in, but that he was watching you and was someday going to *test* you. So I took matters into my own hands."

"So you did tell someone," Jack surmised.

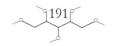

"I couldn't. I hadn't made copies of the journal, so I had no proof – it'd be my word against his," Colonel Clark tried to defend himself. "I did the only thing I could do – watched and waited for the chance to bring him down."

"Which obviously never came," Miranda admonished acidly.

"Wait," I said, the pieces coming together in my mind under the echo of the *in his own hands* part. "They told us his death was ruled an accidental shooting."

"There's no such thing as an accidental shooting involving a soldier with thirty years of service, Clio," Colonel Clark answered, the implication hanging in the air for us all to see.

"Couldn't you come forward then?" Bliss asked, wholly averse to secret-keeping. "He was dead."

"You're forgetting that John died in Colorado when Heigl was still in D.C.," Colonel Clark reminded her. "I knew whomever John had talked to that night was the one who killed him, which meant there had to be someone else involved. But since Heigl didn't name any partners in his journal, I had no way of finding out who the murderer was. I had no choice but to lie low."

"There was nobody you could confide in? Ever?" I asked, even though I thought I already knew the answer.

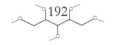

"There was someone," he said, surprising me. "About two years ago, I got a good read on another doctor at Detrick. He was my first potential ally after a decade and a half of living with this alone."

By now, my anger over being lied to was having a hard time fighting off the rush of compassion I couldn't help feeling for this man who'd spent his entire life alone, afraid to trust anyone. He could've told someone, but he didn't want to risk *me*. I'd have to be a heartless witch to fault him for that. He'd been trapped, and he'd chosen the rock over the hard place. I might've done the same thing.

I looked at the foursome behind me, beside me, feeling tremendously grateful that I wouldn't have to know what it was like to go through something like that alone. And even if I couldn't say what I would've done in his shoes, I knew what to do now, in mine.

"And you told him, right?" I guessed, thinking the story'd finally caught up to real time.

"Not quite." Colonel Clark's face fell even further. "I gave him all my notes and he started pulling drug and chemical orders from ninety-one and a few years back to try and piece together what might be in the vitamin cocktail." He needed another deep, deep breath to deliver the tragic news. "But someone must've known he was getting too close to the truth,

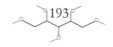

because a few weeks later Dr. Trulle and his wife were killed in another fatal 'accident.' And that's when I found out his daughter was one of Heigl's victims. He never knew."

Oh my God, oh my God, oh my God. My thoughts raced as fast as my pulse. *Trulle. As in Alexis Trulle, from D.C,. whose parents died last year?* It couldn't be any other girl. I turned to reach for Jack, only to find I still hadn't let go of his shoulder from when I'd first latched on. The look in his eyes told me he'd felt the same punch in his gut.

"So how did the information come out?" Garrett probed, either not making the connection to Alexis or, more likely, just needing to push forward.

"I couldn't take any more chances with people's lives, don't you see?" Colonel Clark pleaded. "Other soldiers' or yours." It seemed like retelling the story was re-waking and re-breaking him all over again. "I wanted to go public, but I couldn't be sure of anyone in the chain of command. That's when I went to the press. I knew if the story hit the national stage, there'd be no way to shut it down. And when it blew, I made sure I was right there with the best plan to put into play."

"There was no secret informant." Jack had already put it together, so his statement bore no hint of a question.

"Just me," Colonel Clark admitted for the first time to anyone since he'd leaked the story to the news reporter, and even

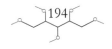

they'd never met face-to-face.

"That makes it sound like it's all over," Miranda said, but her tone clearly indicated that she believed the opposite was the case. For once, I agreed with her.

"Except for finding out the long-term effects of the drug on all of you. You deserve at least that," the colonel replied, looking like he really believed we were that close to a resolution. The five of us shared one look, coming to the silent agreement that Colonel Clark was clearly not running the sinister show behind the scenes, and that now we needed to fill him in on some things.

"Uh, sir?" Garrett went first. "It's not time to come off the field yet; it's still game-on for somebody."

"What he's trying to say," I spoke up to make sense of Garrett's vague sports analogy, "is that there's something going on on campus, and, from what you've just told us, I think it may go all the way back to that unidentified accomplice."

"Have you been threatened?" Colonel Clark moved closer to me, as if compelled to provide physical protection from the possible threat.

Before I could answer, the faint click of a gun hammer being cocked back alerted us to an unexpected guest. My spine went rigid when a voice rang out mockingly, "She has now."

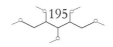

TWENTY

We recognized the threat before the face even came into view; hers was a voice we heard every single day without fail. "Janet," I identified her aloud at the same time she emerged from the shadows, the look on her face nothing less than deliriously victorious.

"Yes it is, my traitorous little mutineers. And Captain Janet is disappointed with all of you, to say the least." I couldn't help but notice how, in true lunatic fashion, she referred to herself in the third person. *If only she'd done that earlier*, I mused, *we'd have called her out and avoided this whole disaster.*

"Captain, I order you to put down your weapon," Colonel Clark commanded, trying to take charge of the situation.

"*Sir*," Janet replied, her voice dripping with sarcasm, "I don't believe you're in a position to be giving orders anymore." He didn't back away, but he also didn't respond. I could only hope that he was biding his time – strategizing, not conceding.

"But why?" Bliss cried, her heartbreak trumping her fear. Where I'd been slowly working toward a friendship with our "mentor," Bliss had jumped into the trust pool with both feet. Now she was drowning in it, and I felt helpless.

"Not as smart as you thought, are you? Even the little know-it-all couldn't figure it out?" Janet sneered at Miranda, then threw a second disdainful look at Jack. "Or the talentless boy-wonder?"

Is this what they mean by break with reality? I wondered, unable to believe the one-eighty flip from the instructor we'd worked with this morning to the crackpot standing in front of us now. Waving her gun around, she was obsessed, possessed, all sessed-out.

"Why don't you fill in us ig'nants, then?" Garrett challenged, either commendably ballsy, or just plain stupid.

The former, it turned out. Once Garrett'd issued the invite, Janet was more than happy to spill her bag of party favors.

"C9x was the most ground-breaking experiment of all time," she praised. "A genetically-altered superforce just waiting for a commander – it's the opportunity of a lifetime!"

"And you think you're the most qualified for the position?" Miranda taunted, not about to let Garrett out-smartmouth her. If she was going down, she sure wasn't going

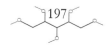

quietly.

"Of course. The esteemed Dr. Heigl," Janet paused after saying his name as if in veneration of a god, "was my father."

"Then why do you have a different last name?" Bliss asked innocently. I swore, she could hear that the world was ending and still focus on the most extraneous thing, like if she had on matching underwear.

But Janet wasn't put off by the irrelevance of the question; she was more than happy to champion herself. "I couldn't very well infiltrate your little camp here with his name, could I? One of my first moves was changing my name when I turned eighteen, before I enlisted."

"You've been planning this since you were a kid?" Even our strategist, Jack, couldn't believe she'd plotted so far ahead.

"I've known my whole life I would carry on my father's work," she asserted, as if there were no more noble cause.

His work? I muttered inwardly. Experimenting on innocent people was some kind of twisted hobby, not a profession.

"You know," Janet changed tack and tone at the same time. "After he died, I would crawl into his closet, between his uniforms, and stay there for hours." *This couldn't be good.*

"That's how I found the journal," confided Janet two-point-oh. "It was hidden in a secret compartment for me to

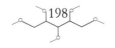

find." She paused to look around the group, her eyes now shining with the hope of the ten-year-old girl she once was. "He wanted me to carry on his legacy."

Legacy, my ass, I retorted to myself. There might still be some part of that lonely little girl in her, but *Captain* Quirk was only concerned with control, power, *glory*. She'd said so herself not two minutes ago.

"You're sick," Colonel Clark said at the end of her speech, his diagnosis coming from a new understanding, almost sympathy.

"Sick? Please." Janet dismissed him quickly and turned to focus on the rest of us. "You whiners should be grateful. I'd have given anything to do what you can do, to have your *abilities*. You don't deserve them."

"Seems to me, then, that we're five superheroes and a colonel and you're all by your itty-bitty ownself," Garrett pointed out.

"Not quite," a new voice called from the shadows. In the second it took me to place it, the other conspirator I'd overheard in this exact same spot came to life. He stepped forward, out of his hiding place, to take his place beside Janet, wielding a matching Beretta. It took me another second to recognize her dark-haired young compatriot, because we'd never officially met.

Garrett didn't need the extra time. "Well, lookie here.

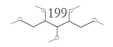

Switch-hitting, Nate?" he sneered, using sarcasm to mask the shock and betrayal of seeing his teammate take the opposing side. The jocks were a small group, the seventeen of them as tight as a real team. Or so we'd thought.

"Hey, man," Nate replied with a nasty smile, "I came here a free agent." It felt like a full-on Scooby Doo moment, where I should've seen it coming, but was instead cartoonishly shocked by the reveal.

Janet smiled affectionately at Nate, as if proud of her pet. "I read all of your files before you got here," she said to us while keeping her eyes on him, "so I knew who I wanted for my inside person. Let's call it *recruiting*."

"Guess that explains how you knew where to get the screw...driver." Garrett threw one hard at Nate.

"Don't be disgusting," Nate shot back. "I had no allegiance to any of you – I didn't even know you. I saw at first-up how this was gonna play out, and I made sure to line up on the winning side. That's it." His words held no hint of guilt or remorse.

"That's a great story...except for the giant hole in the middle," Jack pointed out, ignoring Nate for a moment and returning to Janet. "You weren't even ten years old when John Kaid was killed, which means Heigl had a real partner. Before you."

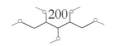

"*Doctor* Heigl, boy. Be respectful of your superiors," Janet sharply corrected Jack before disputing his point. "Sure, he had one ICE guy – some supply officer at Carson. And if that guy'd had half a brain, he might've been of real use. He *ordered* all the pieces, and he still didn't put together what my dad was doing."

"Once my father'd perfected his drug," she went on, "he had no more use for *supply-boy*. Well, except to eliminate John Kaid. Which he did, like a stupid, loyal dog. Then my dad made sure he was never heard from again. The end."

"That'll be you next, dog boy," Garrett told Nate. "Woof, woof."

I suddenly realized that the two gladiators had moved closer to one another with each insult and were now quickly approaching throw-down distance. Someone had to get between them before the tension ignited.

"So what are you going to do with us?" Miranda demanded, clearly not interested in being quieted for one minute, let alone eternity.

"Shoot you, of course," Janet answered flippantly, tilting the gun to remind us it was cocked and ready. "I've got fifteen rounds in here, and I only need six. Seems I'm all set."

"What about your army?" I jumped in, trying to talk her down. "You need us."

"You?" she snorted. "I've got dozens of *you* back at the

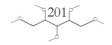

201

dorm." She paused to give Garrett a small frown. "He's a little harder to give up, but there're more where he came from, too."

She didn't say anything for a minute, and I looked over at Bliss, who, it broke my heart to see, was watching Janet with wide-eyed expectancy. Even in the face of danger, of *death*, I could tell that she was waiting for Janet to say that she was special – that she was her *star*.

But it was Jack who spoke next. "Someone will hear," he argued with Janet, sounding far more confident than I felt.

"Si-len-cer," she countered. "Say it with me." And as if I were channeling Bliss, I thought, *Just because you're going crazy doesn't mean you have to be so nasty. 'Kill them with kindness,' isn't that what they say?*

"Isn't there security here?" Miranda piped up, sounding like an indignant celebrity looking for help fending off the paparazzi.

"The guards only secure the perimeter of the compound," Janet assured her. "The inside security team is the training staff – that'd be me. The second line's not coming in unless I send up an SOS, which I will obviously *not* be doing."

I hated that she had an answer to quash every hope we launched, but I wasn't giving up. At least now that we knew we were on our own, we could stop waiting for reinforcements and find a way to help ourselves. I began flash-playing in my mind

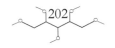

every fight-scene I'd ever watched, trying to think up an action plan. I'd learned enough self-defense to know that we definitely couldn't let her take us deeper into the woods like she surely planned to; the secondary location was always better for your attacker and more dangerous for you than the first.

I tried to do some fast math – five kids and a middle-aged man against two looney-toons with guns – and found the outcome incalculable. We may have special abilities, but none that classified as weapons; I was pretty sure that invisibility and dazzle-ment weren't bullet-proof.

Moving targets are harder to hit, popped into my mind next. *What can we do to just get out of the way?* Miranda and I could vanish and take off, while Garrett could leap up and out into the trees. Sparkling Bliss could maybe throw up a blind long enough for the rest of us to act, but that would only hold Janet off for a second, not take her out. Bliss would still be vulnerable, and Jack fully defenseless. *What to do?*

"Can't we just hug it out?" Garrett was also grasping at straws – relying on humor as his first line of defense.

"People will come looking for us. They won't just let us disappear," Jack also played to his strength – words, calm and rational.

"And I'll tell them you went AWOL," Janet responded, unaffected by either tactic. "That you didn't want to be here

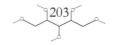

anymore." She had her lines memorized.

"Someone'll be up this path any minute now, headed back to the gym," Garrett tried again, and as much as I hated that he was making himself more of a target, I wanted to kiss him. To kiss all of my friends, actually, for continuing to fight what looked to be an un-winnable battle.

Nate, apparently, wasn't so appreciative of Garrett's spunk, and relished in bursting his bubble. "Dude, today's session was a killer – coach ran us all ragged," he reminded him. "You and I both know that the rest of the guys are going to chow down, hit the showers, then crash or race Wii for hours."

"And we'll need way less time than that to take care of this, don't worry," Janet assured us. "Now let's move it."

"You'll never get away with this," Miranda made a last-ditch effort at stalling. "Somebody will figure it out."

"Right, because they've been so brilliant up until now. The world believes everything the government spoon-feeds them. That's what got you here in the first place, remember?"

"Don't you know who my mom is?" Bliss launched a final attempt of her own, empowered by the importance of her mom's position for the first time in her life.

"She's an idiot," Nate snapped, his insulting tone surprisingly even more personal than he'd used with Garrett. What could Bliss have possibly done to him? *Smiled too sweetly?*

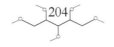

Acted too nice? I didn't have to wait long to find out.

"My father was next in line for that position," he snarled, "and your tramp mother got it because she has boobs. She doesn't deserve it."

So much for being under Janet's spell, I realized. *Looks like somebody's got some serious motive of his own.*

But while I was thinking it through, Bliss was suddenly all-action – flying at Nate in a rage. It was so uncharacteristic of my mild-mannered friend that I wouldn't have believed it if I hadn't seen it. And frame-by-frame.

I didn't know if I was in shock, or if the world had slowed to half-speed. Bliss lunged forward, but in my eyes it happened in stilted increments, as if someone was moving too slowly through a flip-book. Likewise, Nate's eyes widened in fear one degree at a time, his trigger finger following right behind.

Colonel Clark was the only one who seemed to be able to move normally. He'd read the scene before it went down, and heroically dove in front of Bliss a fraction of a second after she took off, using his solid body to block and tackle.

Miranda screamed in horror, seeming to jolt the world back into real-time, and I instinctively ran to the fallen twosome.

"Isn't that touching?" Janet's voice rang out. "Seems like your second dad isn't going to fare any better than your first," she said to me with a bitter laugh as I knelt beside the fallen colonel.

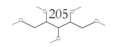

Despite all the commotion, she hadn't moved an inch. Still sure, still steady, still in total control.

Colonel Clark rolled off of Bliss, who sat up looking stunned but unhurt. But now that he was turned over, we could see that the colonel was covered in blood from shoulders to waist, making it impossible to see an entry wound or to know how bad off he was. His breath came out in shallow gasps and he uttered what I could only hope was not a dying declaration. "Clio, your dad would be so proud of you," he said, looking steadily into my eyes before closing his and slipping from consciousness.

"Time's up, folks," Janet interrupted as my chest threatened to collapse in on itself. "Grab the great defender, boys, and let's go." She waved her gun to indicate that she wanted Garrett and Jack to pick up the colonel's limp body and precede her into the woods.

As the guys both moved toward Colonel Clark – and Bliss and me – I saw their eyes lock on each other, trying to communicate a silent plan. *Please let Garrett be better at reading Jack's thoughts than he is at mine,* I pleaded silently.

Then, as if in answer to a different prayer, yet another player joined the game.

"Time *is* up," she said, stepping into view. "For you, Captain Quirk."

"Alexis!" I cried, jumping to her side. I'd never been so

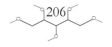

glad to see anyone in my life, and it took all my willpower to keep from hugging her.

"Hey, look who's going for the outside assist," Garrett cheered, grinning widely. "Not that we needed it or anything," he rushed to clarify. "I've totally got things under control here."

"Cut the reunion, kids," Janet snapped, clearly not concerned by the latest addition. "I've got enough shots here for everyone – what's one more lost kid?"

"What's that noise?" Bliss interrupted, the first to hear a whirring sound somewhere high in the sky.

"You fixed the phone signal!" I realized, putting together the aircraft noise and the timing of Alexis's appearance. If it weren't for that stupid wall around her, I'd have grabbed her and jumped up and down that we were actually going to be okay.

"Yup," she confirmed smugly, "and my first call out was to CNN. I knew the news'd get here faster than anyone else." I loved that she'd unknowingly taken a page right out of the colonel's playbook. And hated that he wasn't able to hear it.

"Ooh, I hope they send Anderson Cooper. He's a hottie." Miranda completely detached from the drama at hand and started smoothing her hair and prepping for the cameras.

"You fools," Janet growled. "This campus was specifically designed to be camouflaged from aerial view. You'll be dead before the chopper can find a place to land." But even with her

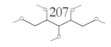

psycho-human arrogance, she couldn't resist one skyward glance.

And that one instant was all Jack and Garrett needed. By silent agreement, they dove simultaneously at our unprepared captors – Jack knocking down Janet from one side and Garrett taking out Nate from the other, throwing them all into a wild scramble for control of the weapons. In the rolling mass of arms and legs, I couldn't see who was on top, who was taking the upper hand, and especially where the guys were in all of it.

Bliss shifted toward Colonel Clark, whether for comfort or to offer protection I wasn't sure, as Miranda, Alexis, and I circled around the wrestling foursome, trying to find some way to help.

And as if an answer to my wish, Janet's hand appeared on the ground in front of me, the glint on the barrel of her gun drawing my eye. I couldn't hesitate and risk it disappearing back into the fray, so I slammed my foot down on her wrist with all my weight. It could only have been better if I'd been wearing one of Alexis's spiky-heeled boots, but Janet still screamed in anguish. Her moment of weakness gave Jack the opening he needed to make a move and he didn't miss a beat.

Hello, Special Forces, I thought as he grabbed hold of her free wrist and pulled it to the one I was still standing on, forcing her face-down into the grass. With his knee driven into her back, pinning her firmly to the ground, Janet finally stopped struggling.

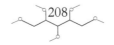

Only when I saw that Jack was safe did I look to see who was winning the other match-up. Garrett had flipped Nate over, too; he'd wrenched Nate's arm behind him and was banging his hand between his shoulders until he dropped the gun. Miranda was right there to snatch it up; then, as if an afterthought, she gave Nate a sharp kick to the ribs before backing out of reach and yelling for help.

I don't know how she knew what I needed, but Alexis moved silently to my side and nudged my foot off Janet's wrist to replace it with her own. I gave her a grateful look before running to where Bliss sat vigil over Colonel Clark to see what I could do for him.

Bliss helped me pull up his shirt to reveal the bloody mess where his stomach was supposed to be. I had to seal my lips and breathe through my nose to keep down the rising vomit and focus. I yanked my own t-shirt over my head and balled it up to press into the wound like I'd seen on TV, trying my best to stem the blood flow while Bliss began compressions on the colonel's chest.

Like a miracle, his eyes fluttered – he was there, but he wasn't. I could hear that the helicopter was no longer circling overhead, but down and somewhere off to our left, rumbling louder than ever. *Are they on the ground?* I thought frantically. *Will they find us in time?* Tears started spilling down my cheeks, and I knew the pain I felt was more than just from witnessing the suffering of another human being. I needed him to be okay, needed to tell him I was sorry....

I was so caught up in the moment that I didn't register the men charging down the path toward us until one moved me out of the way to get a look at the colonel. The other man pulled a walkie-talkie from his pants and rapidly fired off instructions to the chopper to send down the co-pilot with the med-kit and defibulator kept on board.

Then somehow Dr. Larson was on the scene; he must've heard the aerial commotion from far away, then Miranda's screams when he got closer. He was quick to take charge of the situation – directing the two newly-arrived men to pick up Colonel Clark and follow him to the medical center. It hadn't occurred to me before now that Larson must have all the equipment he needed right on campus at the clinic. *But even so, would they get him there in time?*

I stayed rooted to the spot I'd been relocated to by the chopper guys as they took off, kids and staff now swarming to the site from the main buildings. I dazedly watched Garrett's coach cuff Janet, then Nate. Then something was on my head, over my eyes for a second before I could see again.

I'd forgotten I was only in my bra and shorts until Jack took off his own shirt and put it on me to cover me back up. He

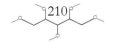

sat down and folded me wordlessly into his arms, knowing instinctively that there was nothing he could say right now to console me, and I finally collapsed into uncontrollable sobs.

TWENTY ONE

*T*he press conference began at eight a.m. on Friday, making it hard to tell if the Army *wanted* to catch viewers before they left for work, of if they were banking on losing most of the American audience to their commute. Not that it mattered much to me. I'd actually gotten to the main building *early* for the viewing, along with everyone else on campus. We all sat as if bound to our chairs, waiting anxiously for the newly-installed projection TV to come to life.

The event was taking place in D.C., not here, because nobody thought that an onslaught of reporters descending on campus was a good idea. And staff and students were also all interestingly in agreement that *our* remaining here was best. For now.

We'd made the collective decision to stay on campus, but

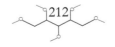

to keep the gates closed. Of course we'd called our parents and all, now that communication had been restored, and the Army'd offered secure escorts out for anyone who wanted to leave, but I didn't know if anyone'd taken them up on it.

No doubt, I wanted to be with my mom – I missed her a ton and knew she'd feel better to see me face-to-face – but I just wasn't ready to go. Not now, and maybe not ever.

Like all of my close friends – and seemingly everyone else, too – there was something about this cocoon we'd woven around ourselves that made leaving a non-choice. I felt as if even sharing this private part of my life with outsiders could fracture its delicate structure. Despite how difficult everything else'd been, the relationships I'd built here were natural, effortless. It didn't matter how long – or short – I'd been here; I'd become a part of this place, these people, and they were now a vital part of me.

Before I could get too sappy, the wall screen came to life and I turned my attention to the surreal-ness of actually *being* the news – the top and only story of the morning.

My old acquaintance Lieutenant Graham commanded the podium and, although I couldn't look away from his direct gaze, I wasn't really listening to his prepared statement. He'd given us all a preview last night before leaving for the capitol. I already knew his summation would inform the American public that a mentally disturbed person had attacked a group of students and an

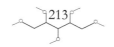

esteemed colonel, but that the perpetrators were now in custody. He used evenly measured words and tone to explain that the immediate threat had passed, but for the sake of those involved – *that'd be us* – security was in place to maintain our safety and anonymity. When he added that C9x research had been temporarily suspended, and that its future remained undetermined at this time, I continued to cling to my belief that he was just telling the viewers what they wanted to hear. Half the reason we'd stayed was to get the answers we'd come for in the first place. The need to find out who we were – *what we were* – hadn't gone away, but Graham and the others weren't talking about our staying on campus after the dust had settled, either.

In keeping with the minimal-information strategy, there was also no mention of Janet's trusty sidekick, Nate, who'd immediately rushed to distance himself from the conspiracy by claiming he'd acted under duress. So as a self-proclaimed "victim" – and one who'd be testifying at Janet's court-marshal hearing – he'd been given immunity by the government. But that didn't mean he was back in circulation with the general population. There were rumors he was still somewhere on campus, but no one knew where; I suspected there may be another building, another secret being kept from us, but that was an intel mission that could wait.

In the corner of the screen, I also saw that Eve Godwin

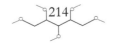

was present at the press conference. She wore her full dress uniform, although she looked more like a supermodel working a USO fashion show than a soldier. I'd heard that if anyone wanted to go public with the details of their experience here at *Camp Solidity*, they'd have to meet with her to prepare an official statement. *No, thanks.* I didn't feel the need to share, particularly with her.

And I especially appreciated that, unlike at Dr. Larson's orientation lecture, Major Godwin didn't need to step in and take over today. Lieutenant Graham was firmly in charge, and watching him deftly field questions, I felt suddenly overwhelmed by the feeling that life had come full circle; this man was the same age my father and Colonel Clark had been when this whole mess began, and I was immediately filled with gratitude for these men who'd watched over me when I hadn't even asked them to, nor thanked them enough for doing so.

For the first time, I also realized how good-looking the lieutenant was. *How'd I miss that?* Maybe it took the big screen to see that if someone were to chisel the all-American man out of granite, they really could do no better than his broad shoulders, high cheekbones, and square jaw. And they'd never be able to capture the glint of his piercing blue eyes. I knew he'd said he was just out of college, but his powerful presence was that of a man in command. *Or maybe*, I thought, only half-joking, *it's just the dress uniform.*

It was no wonder why Colonel Clark had put Lieutenant Graham in charge while he recuperated – seeing the lieutenant like this made it obvious that the colonel would view him as the honorable son he may have had, had his life unfolded differently.

And that made me wonder for the tenth time already this morning how Colonel Clark was doing today. I still hated that he was under Dr. Larson's care, but he'd insisted on staying on campus once he'd gained consciousness and I had to, albeit grudgingly, admit that he did seem well-attended. He was getting stronger every day, due also in large part to a borrowed Wii that he claimed he'd be bowling with by next weekend, so Larson must not be all bad.

I refocused in time to see Lieutenant Graham dismiss the reporters and abandon the microphone bank. Everyone in the great room also began to disperse, except for the six of us.

Yes, six, I thought, so happy that Alexis had now become an integral part of our group. Though she'd initially tried to feign committal to her one-ness, we hadn't allowed her to block us out. And even though she wouldn't admit it, we all knew she was secretly happy to belong. I, for one, was just glad I hadn't missed out on her friendship, not only because she'd saved our lives, but also since the more she opened up, the more I found in her to like.

I turned and regarded this new friend at my side, noticing that she'd worn a deep-violet top instead of her old standard, black. We knew by more than her clothes that the more comfortable she became with us, the more her wall crumbled, and thinking of the unintentional vibe she used to give off, I shivered at how intense her ability must be when she consciously "turned it on."

And if there'd ever been a time for Alexis to wall us out, it would've been after hearing the truth of her parents' deaths. But she'd dealt with the discovery much better than any of us would have – trying to champion their courage instead of returning to grief. She knew that we were all there if she needed to talk, and the fact that this giant mess had taken a parent from me, too, created a bond between us like no other.

As the room emptied, Miranda, Bliss, and Garrett turned around in their seats to face Jack, me, and Alexis in the next row, effectively closing formation. There'd been a lot of talk about post-traumatic stress and counseling from the mentors, or guides, or whatever we were calling them now. But this six-sided circle was all any of us needed.

We'd pretty much closed ranks and made our own small cocoon within the larger one, alternately rehashing what we'd been through, then trying to talk about anything but. Now we'd finally gotten to the point where we had to consider what was

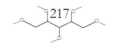

going to happen next. They may not be booting us out today, but I doubted they planned to let us stay forever.

Miranda was the first to broach the dreaded subject. "I don't know about all of you, but I'm stoked to get back to the West Coast sunshine – SPF protected, of course." Her smile faltered and I knew this was going to be a hard conversation if our toughest member couldn't even put up a decent front.

"Right on," Garrett followed suit. "I'm pumped to show off my new skills at ball camp." His grin was a little sunnier, but unfortunately not good enough to lift my spirits right now.

"The timing couldn't be better," I said, giving exuberance my best shot as well. "My mom's here in New York, so if we go home next week, I can join her in the city for the rest of her tour."

"Me, too," Alexis agreed. "New York, I mean. I'll be back at Juilliard in time for summer session – there's a drum symposium I was worried about missing. Guess that's not going to be the case...," she trailed off, a bit wistfully.

"Looks like I'm the only one with no big summer plans. I didn't want to make any until I saw how this all played out, you know?" Jack spoke up, honest but not looking for sympathy.

"Back home for a quiet summer for me, too," Bliss added softly. She paused for a long moment, then practically shouted, "I'm going to miss this place!"

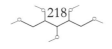

And her admission was all it took to turn our thoughts toward what each of us would miss most, besides each other.

"Yeah, I'm sure not going to find a gym like this one on the prairie," Garrett admitted. "No run-for-your-life, bullet-dodging workouts out there, either," he added with a smirk.

"Really, if they'd just put in a pool and hot tub, this place wouldn't be *that* bad." Miranda gave her opinion with a shrug.

"Yeah, and you all turned out to be not so bad, after all," Alexis tossed out a light jab of her own.

I wanted to jump into the banter as well, but for the first time in my known memory I was all out of quips, jokes, and sarcasm. There was nothing swirling around my brain besides a mush-miasma, and I was afraid if I let it out, it'd come with watery eyes and a runny nose.

It was more than the enormity of what we'd done – unearthing the sadistic plot against us and, together, taking down the homicidal mastermind behind it. That all but faded into the background behind the joy of finding four fantastic new friends, each so uniquely important to me. And then there was *Jack*, for whom I was tumbling head over heels – half the time literally, due to the unfortunate ineptitude of both my brain and tongue. I flicked my glance his way, just for an instant, and found his eyes waiting for mine, as if he'd been reading my thoughts. *How could I possibly walk away from you?* I thought, feeling my heart and

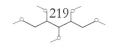

stomach switch places.

The cumulative fatigue seemed to hit all of us at the same time and we reluctantly climbed out of our seats, crossed the now too-quiet room, and made our way outside. Upon exiting the building, we found that the skies had finally opened up, dumping a deluge of water. For the past two days, it'd been like Mother Nature was in limbo with us, hanging her pensive clouds over our heads. And now that our situation had broken, she'd been able to release her pressure valve, too.

Garrett and Bliss, followed by Alexis and Miranda, took off like teams in a mad dash for the dorms, but Jack and I held back, lingering in the shelter of the doorway. "So what now?" Jack asked, and I knew he was asking more than if I was ready to race across the courtyard.

"I think I'm going to write a song," I answered, the words surprising me. I hadn't even known I wanted to, but once it was out there, it made sense. "It's not like I planned to – it's kind of writing itself," I explained, looking down and feeling a bit vulnerable.

"Can we make it a duet? I play the guitar," he offered, gently putting his hands on my hips and drawing me closer to him.

Of course you do – you do everything, I thought.

When I didn't say anything, he ducked his head to find

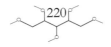

my downward gaze, calling my eyes to his without words. "Seriously, we'll work something out. I'm not going to just let you disappear."

"Bad pun," we both said and smiled at the same time.

Before I could stop myself, I followed up unthinkingly with, "Jinkies." He cocked one questioning eyebrow, and I tried to explain why I'd ruined yet another perfect moment. "It's something my mom and I used to say when I was little – *Jinkies, hook pinkies, and make a wish.*" I looked away as I felt the heat rising in my cheeks. *Was I ever going to stop saying goofy things?*

He put one finger on my chin to turn my face back to his. "Hey," he said softly, "I've got nothing against wishes."

I looked into his shining brown eyes, feeling his easy warmth encircle me, and I wanted to be nowhere else but in this exact space at this very moment in time with this amazing boy. He didn't have to pull me up to him or lean too far down to kiss me; our lips just came together in the natural middle, and all my worries vanished. My hands found their way to the back of his neck and I kissed him with no reservation. I knew now that I wasn't going anywhere, wasn't letting go of this. We'd find a way to work things out, because what we had was real, *Solid.*

A SNEAK PEEK AT THE NEXT
BOOK IN THE "SOLID" SERIES:

SETTLING

*B*y none of my own volition, I abandoned my chair to meet him in his – uninvited maybe, but not unwelcome. One minute I'd been seated, steady; the next I was traversing the gap between us without touching down. All I knew was that there'd been nothing but air supporting me until I'd climbed onto his lap and connected with the solidness of him.

His response to my assault was not immediate; he clutched the armrests as long as conceivably possible while waging an inner battle between desire and decorum. His conflict – his call to me held in check by his uncertainty – froze his body as if he were petrified. More likely not so much by me as by this new *us*.

Breaking his resistance, I ran my hands up his shoulders to touch his fine hair, prickly soft under my fingertips. On his lap, facing him, I nudged up his chin, making him look into my eyes and see that this was what I wanted, what I needed. Our faces a breath apart, I felt heady inhaling his delicious scent. My heart raced even faster, calling his to match pace. My hunger for him burst forth in an intensity I'd never experienced as I claimed the first kiss.

So this is why Eve was the slandered one, the seductress, I thought. That first taste of him, like the first bite of the apple, was the drop that knocked down the floodgates. And in the same instant that I knew there was no going back, that nothing could stop the wave I was riding, he stopped fighting and met me at its crest, joined me in the *us*.

His hands moved smoothly from the armrests to my waist, his broad fingers spreading across my lower back as he settled me more securely onto the seat. My knees slid up to his hips, my legs still folded underneath me but now pressing against the outside of his. And then it was he who deepened the kiss, hurtling from concession to conviction, clutching my backside as I bowed deeper into his chest.

Without fully separating, we both took a necessary gasp at the same instant, seeming to breathe in the same pocket of air, resealing our lips with yet more urgency. *Where did the air come from when desire bound you too tightly to each other to part for even a second? More than just I want you, but I need you – need you more than air?*

As if from a distance, I heard my own throaty moans, vaguely aware I should be embarrassed by the near-growling, but his grip only tightened at the sound. The heat between us climbing higher, his hands followed suit, up my back and sides all at once, over my bursting ribcage, rounding the tops of my shoulders, trailing down to rest lightly on the front of my biceps in an unexpected but tender hold. I wanted the moment to last forever. He was so strong yet soft, vulnerable and safe all at the same time. So intense, so overwhelming, so *not Jack.*

SHELLEY WORKINGER was born in Maine, educated in New Orleans, currently resides in New Jersey, and considers all of them home. "Solid" is her first series.

VISIT HER AT:
WWW.SHELLEYWORKINGER.COM

12284684R10135

Made in the USA
Lexington, KY
03 December 2011